Something is very wrong in the middle pasture. . . .

All at once I noticed that Slim was staring at something down by the creek. "Say, that's a heifer. What's she doing in this pasture?"

A heifer in the home pasture? "Come on Drover," I yelled, "we've got a trespasser! Follow me and sound the alarm!"

The heifer was walking and bawling and looking around for something. Slim watched her for a long time, drumming his fingers on the steering wheel. "I hope I'm wrong, boys, but I got a feeling that we'll find her calf dead in the middle pasture. We may have a killer coyote loose on the ranch."

Murder in the Middle Pasture

John R. Erickson

Illustrations by Gerald L. Holmes

Maverick Books, Inc.

This one is dedicated to
the Ellzeys of Wolf Creek.

MAVERICK BOOKS
Published by Maverick Books, Inc.
P.O. Box 549, Perryton, TX 79070
Phone: 806.435.7611
www.hankthecowdog.com

First published in the United States of America by Maverick Books, Inc. 1984,
Texas Monthly Press, 1988, and Gulf Publishing Company, 1990.
Subsequently published simultaneously by Viking Children's Books and Puffin
Books, members of Penguin Putnam Books for Young Readers, 1999.
Currently published by Maverick Books, Inc., 2011.

3 5 7 9 10 8 6 4

LIBRARY OF CONGRESS CATALOGING-IN-PUBLICATION DATA
Erickson, John R.
[Hank the Cowdog and murder in the middle pasture]
Murder in the middle pasture / John R. Erickson ; illustrations by Gerald L. Holmes.
p. cm. — Hank the Cowdog ; 4.
Originally published: Hank the Cowdog and murder in the middle pasture.
Summary: When a calf is murdered, Hank, a wiley cowdog and head of ranch
security, pursues a gang of wild dogs and a clan of coyotes to find the killer.
ISBN 1-59188-104-8 (pbk.)
[1. Dogs—Fiction. 2. Mystery and detective stories. 3. West (U.S.)—Fiction.
4. Humorous stories.] I. Holmes, Gerald L., ill. II. Title. III. Series: Erickson, John
R. Hank the Cowdog ; 4.
PZ7.E72556Mu 1999 [Fic]—dc21 98-41854 CIP AC

Hank the Cowdog® is a registered trademark of John R. Erickson.

Printed in the United States of America

CONTENTS

CHAPTER ONE

The Case of
the Wild Hogs

It's me again, Hank the Cowdog. On December 19, we got a snow. On December 20, it snowed again. On December 21 the overflow of the septic tank froze up, making it impossible for me to bathe.

By December 22 we had four inches of snow on the ground and fellers, it was cold. It was that morning, at approximately 9:00 o'clock, that I awoke from a deep sleep and noticed something very peculiar.

My bed was shaking.

My bed consisted of two old gunnysacks and under normal conditions it didn't shake. Something strange was afoot, and it was my job to check it out.

1

I opened one eye, perked one ear, and I sniffed the air. In the security business we call this a preliminary scan. In other words, at that point I wasn't using all my sensory equipment. There's no sense in squandering your gifts, no matter how many you have.

Well, I sniffed and I looked and I listened. I smelled diesel fuel but I always smelled diesel in my bedroom because the tank on the north side leaked and the cowboys on our outfit were too lazy to fix it. Now, if they'd had a fuel leak in THEIR bedrooms, they would have fixed it pronto, but this was only Hank's bedroom so nobody was worried about it.

Anyway, I sniffed and I looked and I listened. And then I heard it: a strange grunting sound. And my bed was shaking again. I had no choice but to open my other eye and put my other ear into service.

I scanned the area from horizon to horizon and suddenly realized that there was something in my bed—something small, white, short-haired, and stub-tailed.

"Drover?"

"Uhhh."

"Drover?"

"Huh?"

"Get out of my bed."

"What?" He lifted his head and stared at me. His eyes were out of focus. "Hank, is that you?"

"Who else would be in my bed at this hour?"

"I don't know. Oh Hank, I had a terrible dream!"

"You're fixing to have a genuine nightmare if you don't get your carcass out of my bed."

"I dreamed we had snow on the ground and it was bitter cold and I was freezing and . . ." He looked around. "Oh my gosh, my dream's come true."

"This is your lucky day, son. Now scram."

He raised up and stood there shivering. "Oh Hank, I'm so cold and miserable! Let me stay in bed with you where it's warm."

"No dice. Did you know that you grunt in your sleep?"

He stared at me. "Grunt?"

"That's right. You're worse than a bunch of hogs. A guy can't sleep with all that nonsense going on in his bed."

"No, that wasn't me, Hank, honest it wasn't. I woke up in the night and I could have sworn I saw," he rolled his eyes around and dropped his voice to a whisper, "a bunch of hogs—right over there!"

"Do you expect me to believe that?" He nodded. I chuckled. "Well, I've got news for you, Drover. I don't believe anything I hear and only half of what I see, so there's very little chance that I'll swallow your story."

"Well, okay. Sure was a good one though."

"I'm sure it was. Now, if you'll just . . . were they wild hogs or domestic?"

"Wild."

"Nonsense. We don't have wild hogs around here. What makes you think they were wild?"

"Well, they had big long white things . . ."

"We call them tusks. Go on."

"And wicked red eyes . . ."

"Hm. Keep going."

"And four legs . . ."

"That fits."

"And they were grunting, Hank."

"Wait a minute, hold it. They were grunting?"

"Yeah, they sure were. Does that mean any-thing?"

"Possibly so, Drover, but before we jump to any hasty conclusions, I have one last question. It is possible that they released a type of odor from their musk glands that smelled exactly like diesel fuel?"

He rolled his eyes. "I think maybe they did, Hank, I'm almost a hundred percent sure they did."

"Well, there we are, Drover. Now that I've managed to drag the testimony out of you, what we have here is the Case of the Wild Hogs."

"Wild hogs! Oh my gosh!"

"Yes indeed. They're armed with enormous tusks and extremely dangerous. You ever go one-on-one against a wild hog?"

"Heck no."

"Well, let me tell you, they're bad mocus. They can rip your guts out with one slash. They can chew your ears off with one bite. They're fast, they're quick, they're utterly heartless."

"Oh!"

"Our first objective is to find out what they're doing on this ranch without permission. Our second objective is to run 'em off the ranch without getting ourselves cut up into a dozen pieces."

"What are we gonna do?"

"I just happen to have a plan."

"Thank goodness!"

"If you'll shut your little yap and let me finish."

"Okay."

I drew out the battle plan in the snow. "We're here at Point Abel. Over here we have Point Baker and over here Point Charlie. As you can see, the three points form a triangle."

"Oh."

"I'll proceed to Point Baker, over here, and then sneak over to Point Charlie, right here. We'd best hold you in reserve here at Point Abel."

"You mean . . . I have to stay here and guard the gunnysacks? You won't let me get out in the snow?"

"That's correct. When it comes to tracking wild hogs, we use only the first string."

"Oh drat."

"If you see anything suspicious, sound the alarm. You got all that?" He nodded. "All right, that covers it. Good luck. I'll be in communication."

At that moment, I spotted Pete the Barncat up by the yard fence. He rubbed up against the corner post and he was purring like a little motorboat.

How do you suppose a cat does that? I've tried it a hundred times and I've never been able to purr.

I loped up the hill to check him out.

"Morning, Hankie. Did you find any monsters in the night?"

"Funny you should ask. As a matter of fact, yes, and I've got some questions for you."

"Oh good. I just love to answer questions."

"Number one, did you see any wild hogs around here in the early morning hours?"

"Hmmm, wild hogs. How many?"

"I don't know, four, five, six?"

"No. I didn't see four, five, or six."

"How many did you see?"

"Seven."

"Why didn't you say so?"

"Well, you asked if I saw . . ."

"Never mind what I asked! What we're after is right answers, not right questions. It doesn't take any brains to ask the right question, but I wouldn't expect a cat to know that. Which way were they going?"

"Who?"

"The wild hogs, you dunce."

"Oh." He licked one of his paws. "Which way do you think they were going?"

"East."

"That's right, Hankie. You're pretty sharp."

"You may have been crazy when you got here, cat, but you're talking sense now. That's all for the moment, but don't leave the ranch. I may have some more questions for you."

He grinned. "Any time, Hankie. Good luck with the wild hogs." Off he went, twitching the end of his tail back and forth.

I never did like that twitching business. Really gets under my skin, makes me mad.

I headed east and made a patrol. Didn't turn
up any clues, no tracks, nothing. An hour later I
arrived back at the command post. I found Drover
asleep on my bed. I gave him a rude awakening.

"Wake up, get out of my bed, and listen, in
that order."

"Okay, Hank, what did you find?"

"We had seven head of wild hogs go through
here sometime after midnight."

Drover gasped. "Did you find 'em?"

"Not exactly. Wild hogs are very clever. They
managed to hide their tracks, but you'll notice

that they left their scent behind. Smell."

Drover sniffed the air. "Diesel fuel?"

"That's what they wanted us to think, but we're one step ahead of them, aren't we? The bottom line, Drover, is that they passed through the ranch in a big hurry, probably in fear of their lives. As far as I'm concerned, we've solved the case."

"Whew! Boy, I was scared there for a while."

"Even I had a few tense moments, Drover. Wild hogs are nothing to sneeze at."

Drover sneezed. "Oh, I'm so cold!"

I studied the runt for a long time, trying to decide if he was trying to be funny or if this was a clue that might open up a new conspiracy. After much deliberation, I decided that he had merely sneezed.

Case closed.

CHAPTER TWO

How Was I Supposed to Know She Didn't Want Me to Go?

Solving a major case in an hour was nothing out of the ordinary for me. I mean, when you get into your higher echelon of cowdogs, brains and breeding and dashing good looks are standard equipment.

Your common unpapered ranch mutt might have one quality out of the three, but not all three at once. Where I solved the Wild Hog Case in an hour's time, your ordinary mutt would spend a day and a half on it.

Your sub-ordinary mutt, such as Drover, might

take a month and a half to crack the case.

Well, I had cracked the case and felt that warm glow of satisfaction that comes when a dog knows he's done his job, yet the investigation had taken its toll and I was ready to throw up a long line of Z's.

I kicked Drover out of my bed, fluffed it up, and was in the process of turning around in a tight circle, looking for the perfect spot to land, when I heard the sound of a motor.

I froze. My ears shot up. A snarl came to my lips. I looked to the left. I looked to the right. And then I saw it. A pickup was pulling into the gravel drive behind the house, and the gravel was popping under the weight of the tires.

The intruder parked beside Sally May's car, which may have been a significant clue. On the other hand, it may have meant nothing. A guy doesn't know until . . . you get the idea.

"Get up, Drover, that pickup hasn't been cleared."

"But Hank . . . do we have to run in the snow?"

I gave him a withering glare. "Unless you can fly, son, you'll have to run in the snow. Come on."

With a look of agony stamped on his face, Drover ventured one foot into the snow. I streaked past him and headed up the hill to check the tires on that unidentified pickup.

Turned out to be Slim's rig so there was no real emergency, but just to be on the safe side, I restamped his right front tire. There's no sense in taking chances.

High Loper and Sally May came out the back door. Loper had two suitcases in each hand and a playpen under his arm. Sally May carried the baby and several packages wrapped in colorful paper and tied with ribbons.

I sat down beside the gate and hung around to see what was going on. Drover had made it up the hill by that time. He stood shivering in the snow with his feet together.

Loper appeared to be in a foul mood and Slim started joshing him. "Gosh, Loper, I sure wish I was going someplace for Christmas. You sure y'all got enough stuff. You forgot the dinner table and the commode."

Sally May gave him the evil eye. "Slim, this isn't the time for your brand of humor. When you get married and have kids, you'll understand about traveling."

"Yes ma'am."

When Sally May wasn't looking, Loper shook his head at Slim and his mouth formed the words, "No you won't."

Slim shoved his hands into his jeans pockets and grinned at Loper. "Reckon that stuff'll fit into the car or do you want me to hook up the stock trailer?"

Loper muttered under his breath, something about "your Sunday britches." I studied Slim's jeans. They looked normal to me—kind of worn and dirty, actually, and I sure wouldn't have described them as church clothes. But cowboys are a strange breed. They don't always think like the rest of the world.

I was waiting beside the gate when Sally May came out. I wagged my tail and gave her a big cowdog smile. She looked down at me with narrowed eyes and said, "Get away, you nasty thing!"

What . . . ? How . . . ? Hey, I didn't jump up on her, I didn't lick her in the face, I didn't lick her on the leg. I didn't do anything but smile at her!

All right, maybe she was still sore at me for jumping up on the dinner table and eating those T-bone steaks, or for running into the utility room after I'd been sprayed by a skunk, but heck, that had been months ago.

I was perfectly willing to start over with a clean slate and try to make something of the friendship, but Sally May had always been bad about carrying a grudge. Over little things too.

So she walked past me with her nose in the air, and then you know what she did? On her way to the car she saw Mister Pitiful, Mister Half-Stepper, Mister Sleep-Till-Noon—meaning Drover, of course—and instead of saying "Get away you nasty thing," she bent down and rubbed his neck.

"Poor puppy's cold." She straightened up. "Oh Slim, why don't you let Drover sleep in the utility room while we're gone. Poor little thing doesn't have a warm coat like," she looked at me and her lip curled up, "like Hank McNasty."

I wagged my tail.

"Hank can stay out with the skunks and the sewer, but Drover needs a warm bed."

Let me intrude here to make one small point. Drover had very little promise as a cowdog, but even if he'd had papers and instincts and the rest of the program, that kind of mollycoddling would have ruined him.

The worst thing you can do to a ranch dog is spoil him. Let him stay inside in the winter and you've ruined him. For the rest of his life, he'll expect a warm bed.

Maybe I'm old-fashioned, but I still believe that a cowdog ought to be just a little tougher than your ordinary breeds, and you'll never catch me sleeping in a warm house, no matter how cold it gets outside.

So there you are, a little insight into the price we pay for being special, and also a little insight into why Drover would never go far in the business.

In addition to being dumb and chickenhearted, he had a weakness for comfort.

Sally May opened the back door of the car. Then she opened the front door too and put the baby into the baby seat. I watched from the gate.

Why had she opened both the doors? Why had she left the back door open? Was she trying to tell me something? Was it possible that . . . ?

I studied on that. It finally dawned on me that she was giving me an opportunity to go on the trip with them. What else could it mean?

Women are pretty subtle. They don't always come out and tell you what's on their minds. Often they will say one thing and then turn around and do another. A guy has to stay alert and interpret the signs.

Why did she want me to go with them on the trip? Maybe by the time she reached the car, she'd thought things over and decided she wanted extra protection for the baby. That made sense. I mean, it's common knowledge that in spite of our gruff exterior, we cowdogs are very protective of children.

Well, I can tell you that I had other things to do. I had about two weeks' work lined up and going off on a trip really didn't fit into my program. But a guy can't ignore the call of duty.

If Sally May wanted me to go, by George I had to go. So I hopped into the car and sat down in the backseat.

Her eyes came up and stabbed me. Her nostrils flared. "Get your dirty paws out of my car! Scat, shoo! Loper, come get your dog out of the backseat!"

Huh?

Loper appeared at the door. "Dang it, Hank, get out of the car."

Now wait a minute . . .

"Come on, boy, out. Don't we have enough trouble getting away on a trip without you?"

I whapped my tail on the seat and looked from one face to the other. I didn't know what to do.

"He's getting mud all over the seat!"

"Hank, for crying out loud! Come on, get out."

Loper reached in, grabbed me by the scruff of the neck, and pitched me into the snow. He aimed a boot at my tail end, but I got out of the way, just in time.

I don't know how you please these people. One minute they want you to . . . never mind.

At last they got the baby and the luggage loaded. Slim came out to say good-bye. "Y'all have a good time, and don't worry about the ranch. Me and Hank'll take care of everything."

Loper laughed and shook his head. I didn't see anything funny about that.

"Keep an eye on those heavy heifers. They'll start calving any day now. And try to keep the house halfway nice. We don't want to come home to a wreck."

"You just have a good Christmas and don't worry about a thing," said Slim.

They shook hands and Loper climbed into the car. As he was backing out the driveway, Loper looked at me and shook his head. I wagged my tail and barked the car all the way up to the county road.

The car tires rumbled over the cattle guard and they were gone. I trotted back down to the house. Big soft flakes of snow were falling from the . . . well, from the sky, of course. I was ready to knock off and get some sleep, but on my way down to the gas tanks I heard a terrible racket up at the machine shed.

It sounded like a dogfight. One of the dogs involved was Drover, and unless my ears deceived me, he was coming out on the short end of the tussle.

Outlaws
on the Ranch

I loped up the hill to the machine shed. By the time I got there, the fight was over. Drover had disappeared, and standing over our dog bowl (actually, it was an old Ford hubcap turned upside down) was a dog I'd never seen before.

He was eating our dog food.

I didn't like his looks. He was a big dude—tall, pretty wide in the shoulders but skinny everywhere else, covered with long scruffy hair, had a notch out of his left ear and dark spots around his eyes. I couldn't tell about his breeding. Appeared to me he might have had a little German police, a little cowdog, and maybe a touch of greyhound in him.

He looked pretty rough, but what bothered me

most about him was the way he'd made himself at home with our dog food. Instead of running away when he saw me coming, he raised his head, glared at me, and went back to eating.

"I'm borrowing some of your dog food, pal. Hope you don't mind."

"A lot of dogs ask permission before they move in and eat someone else's food."

He shrugged. "You was busy."

"You could have waited."

"I was hungry." He stopped chewing and lifted his head. "Anyways, I don't like to beg."

"Asking and begging are two different things."

"I'll remember that." He went on with his eating.

I walked around in front of him, sizing him up. "I'll need to check your identification."

He laughed at that. "Identification! Who do you think you are, pal?"

"Hank the Cowdog, Head of Ranch Security."

He stopped chewing and studied me. "So what do you want me to do? Faint?"

"You can start with your name."

"Buster."

"Where are you from and what are you doing on this ranch?"

"Let's just say that I'm from a place where it

ain't polite to ask too many questions, and I'm passing through."

"How long you plan to be on the ranch?"

"Until I leave."

"In that case, you won't be here long. Finish your meal and move on."

He leaned his head toward me. "Shove off, cowdog. You're liable to give me indigestion."

I didn't like that and my first instinct was to jump him. But I held back. "Where's Drover?"

"Who? Oh, the flunky? I slapped him around a little bit and he hid in the barn." He arched his brows. "That ain't a bad idea, hiding in the barn

when Buster comes around. A lot of dogs didn't and they ain't with us anymore. Study your lessons on that, pal."

I walked up to him and stared him in the eyes. "It's time for you to hit the road. We don't have a place for stray dogs."

"Stray dogs!" He threw his head back and laughed at that. "Hey boys, did you hear that? The Head of Ranch Security thinks we're stray dogs!"

All at once the weeds at the west end of the machine shed moved and out stepped three more dogs. They weren't as big as Buster, but they looked just as tough and scroungy. At that same moment, Drover's nose poked out the machine shed door.

"Hank, be careful! He's got a gang with him."

"Thanks a lot, Drover. As usual, your timing wasn't too swift."

The thugs swaggered out of the weeds and formed a semi-circle behind Buster. One of them, a short stocky dog with one of those pushed-in bulldog-type faces, spoke up.

"I'll take him, boss, just say the word."

"Easy, Muggs. I'm still eating my breakfast." He took another bite and looked around. "Pretty nice layout you got here. If I was inclined to honest work, I might be interested in this job. But

I ain't much inclined to honest work, am I Muggs?"

Muggs thought that was funny. "Har, har, har! You sure ain't, boss. You're the most dangerous killer and thief in Ochiltree County."

Buster glanced at me. "You hear that, pal? This is your lucky day. You're in the presence of a living legend. You got any cats around here?"

"Maybe and maybe not. Why?"

"I'm still hungry. And when I'm hungry I get mad easy. Muggs, scout around and see if you can find me a cat."

"Sure, boss." Muggs stepped out but I moved into his path.

"Hold it right there. Any cats on this ranch belong to me. We've got no free cats."

Muggs stopped. "Hey, boss, the jerk says he's got no free cats. You want that I should slap him around?"

Buster came over to where I was. "Listen, pal, maybe you didn't understand. See, I'm very dangerous. I got this terrible temper and when I don't get my way I just lose my head. Just ask Muggsie about it." There was a moment of silence. "Go on, Muggs, tell him."

"You told him to ask, boss, and he didn't ask."

"Okay, so ask him something, pal."

"All right," I said. "Muggs, do you know the difference between a duck?"

"Uh . . . a duck and what?"

"Just a duck, that's all."

"Naw. What's the difference between a duck?"

"One leg's the same."

The other two guys laughed at that. Muggs glanced over at them and then his eyes came back to me.

"I don't get that, man. Is that a joke or something?"

"You didn't get it?"

"Naw . . . well . . . uh say the last part one more time."

"One leg's the same."

"Oh yeah! Har, har, har. Yeah, one leg's the same, okay, I get it now." Muggs and the other two laughed it up. But Buster didn't.

"Hey Muggs? That was a stupid joke. You laughed at a stupid joke. It's stupid to laugh at stupid jokes." He came over to me and poked me in the chest with his paw. "You're making my boys look stupid, pal. Now tell me where the cats are."

"I told you. We got no free cats."

"Okay, Muggs. He's all yours. Work him over."

"Sure, boss." Muggs rolled his shoulders and pawed the snow. "You're gonna get it now, fella, 'cause you made me laugh at a stupid joke."

"Hey Muggs, have you heard the latest knock-knock joke?"

"Naw, how's it go?"

"Well, you say knock-knock."

"Okay. Uh, knock-knock."

"Who's there?"

"Uh . . . Muggs."

"Muggs who?"

He stared at me for a long time. "Uh . . . Muggs the dog."

I shook my head. "That wasn't so good, Muggs. Let's try another one."

"Okay. Knock-knock."

"Who's there?"

"What do I say now?"

"What-do-I-say-now who?"

"No, no, uh time out for a minute. What do I say now?"

"That wasn't so good either. Let's try another one. Knock knock."

"Uh, who's there?"

"Drover."

"Drover who?"

"Drover, run get Slim and hurry." I cackled. "You didn't get that? DROVER, RUN GET SLIM AND HURRY, get it?"

"Oh-h-h-h, yeah, I get it now, okay. Har, har, har."

Buster had been listening but hadn't said a word or cracked a smile. "Wait a minute, wise guy. I don't get it. What do you mean 'run get slim and hurry'?"

Out of the corner of my eye, I saw Drover slink out of the machine shed. I moved in closer to Buster so he wouldn't notice.

"Well, slim means trim, thin, un-fat, skinny. You might say that a pencil is slim but not a watermelon. Get it?"

"Naw. I think you're telling another stupid joke."

"All right, let's try another one. Knock-knock."

Muggs started to answer but Buster stopped him. "Back off, Muggs, I'll handle this myself. Who's there?"

"Thereesa."

"Thereesa who?"

I shot a glance over my shoulder and saw Slim walking up the hill. "Thereesa cowboy coming this way and he hates stray dogs."

Muggs and the other two laughed. I guess they would have laughed at anything. But Buster just glared at me. "I still don't get it, pal, and I'm sick of your stupid jokes."

"Hey boss," said Muggs in a whisper. "There IS a cowboy coming. It ain't no joke."

"Then why were you laughing, you idiot!"

Muggs hung his head. "I don't know. It seemed funny at the time, and the other guys laughed too."

"You're all idiots. Okay, wise guy," he turned to me, "you won this round but we'll meet again. You'll be sorry, pal, believe me. Come on, boys, let's scatter!"

They took off in a high lope, streaked past the hay lot, and then headed north toward the canyons.

When Slim got to the machine shed, he took off his hat and scratched his head, as if he couldn't figure out what Drover had gotten so excited about. Then he saw the empty hub cap and said, "Oh, you're out of food."

He filled it up and went back to work.

Me and Drover stayed in front of the machine shed. He was shivering again. "Well, Drover, what do you have to say for yourself? You let me walk right into a trap. I could have been mauled by those apes. Why didn't you warn me?"

"Well . . . I tried."

"You tried to disappear, is what you tried to do. You ran into the machine shed to save your own skin. Can you think of any reason why I shouldn't write this up and put it in your file?"

"Well . . . my leg was hurting."

"That'll sound good in my report, son: 'He let four stray dogs take over the ranch but his leg was hurting.' Do you think you could get a job on another ranch with that kind of report?"

He lowered his head and started crying. "I was scared, Hank, I was just terrified. You don't understand. You've never been a little mutt. Oh Hank, don't write me up!"

"What else can I do? What would you do if you were Head of Security and found that you had a chicken-hearted little mutt on your staff?"

"Well . . . I'd make him stand in the corner for two whole hours."

"Two hours, huh? That might . . ."

"And I'd make him stand in the corner in the machine shed."

"Why the machine shed?"

"Because it has corners, four of 'em."

"Hmm. That's true. A guy can't stand in the corner if there isn't a corner."

"That's what I mean."

"I know that's what you mean. That's what I said."

"I know that's what you said that's what I mean. That's what I said."

"No, that's what I said, and on this ranch what I say is what counts. Now get your little self into the machine shed and stand in the corner for two hours."

"Oh Hank, not the machine shed!"

"Yes, the machine shed. And while you're standing in the corner, I want you to think about Life."

"Life?"

"Yes sir, every bit of it."

"Okay, Hank, but this seems awful cruel." He walked through the snow and into the machine shed.

I went on down to the corrals to make the rounds, check things out. Maybe it was cruel, making little Drover stand in the corner for two whole hours, but handing out stern sentences just goes with the territory when you're Head of Ranch Security.

CHAPTER FOUR

Attacked by
a Horned Moron

Ordinarily, Slim stayed in a little camp house down the creek a ways, but Sally May and Loper must have asked him to stay in their place while they were gone on the trip.

Well, that afternoon, while Drover was doing his time in the machine shed corner, I went with Slim and helped him with the feeding. We fed alfalfa hay to those cattle up in the north pastures.

Slim loaded most of the hay. Actually, he loaded all of the hay, but when he got down to the bottom tier of bales, I made a hand. Every time he moved one of the bottom bales, I was right there, ready to pounce on the rats that lived there.

It's pretty impressive, what I can do to a rat. I mean, the human race has spent hundreds of years looking for a better mousetrap, but in the rat department the whole matter was settled the day cowdogs were invented.

There's no better rat killer than a highly trained, highly conditioned, highly intelligent cowdog.

In just a matter of minutes, I notched up four head of rats and also got bit on the lip, which is something a rat will do, bite the tar out of you, and it takes a little of the fun out of it. But I've never been the kind of dog who worried much about his lips.

We got the hay loaded. As I recall, it was stacked about five-high on the pickup, and as usual I scrambled up to the top of the load. That's where I ride. A lot of dogs will try to weasel their way into the cab and ride inside where it's warm. Me, I've always figgered that I could do more good up on top where I can see the country and, you know, keep an eye on things.

Sure, it's cold up there but that's just the price you pay for being on top. I mean, if you can't take it maybe you ought to look around for a bird dog job.

So off we went, driving north into a stiff north wind. That wind was colder than you might suppose. It cut me clean to the bone, and fellers, I was

freezing my tail off! It was a good thing Drover hadn't come along. He'd have been moaning and crying and . . .

Whose idea had it been for Drover to stand in the corner in the machine shed where it was warm and dry? Surely it had been my idea because I'm not easily swayed by what others say, but on the other hand . . .

I was freezing my frazzling tail off in that wind—oh, it must have been sweeping down them canyons at seventy, eighty miles an hour, and I'm talking about blowing snow and icicles and slow death along with it, the kind of creeping cold that can freeze the tongue in your mouth and turn your insides into a solid block of ice in a matter of minutes.

So when Slim stopped the pickup and got out to open the middle pasture gate, I staggered off the load and . . . well, decided that I could serve the ranch better by helping Slim with the driving.

I wouldn't call that weaseling a ride. There's certain times and certain situations when . . .

Look, I wouldn't have done the ranch any good if I'd stayed up there and got myself froze into a solid block of ice. Sometimes a guy has to compromise his principles, but there's a difference between compromising and weaseling a ride.

Anyway, Slim needed help with the driving. He'd get to looking for cattle and forget to watch the road. He went into the ditch three times and hit several holes. Good thing I was there or we might have ended up at the bottom of a canyon.

We parked on a hill in the middle pasture and Slim rolled down his window and called the cattle. He cupped his hand around his mouth and hollered, "Wooooooo!" in a loud, high-pitched voice. Kind of hurt my ears, to tell you the truth, and it sure was funny the way his Adam's apple moved up and down.

The first-calf heifers were in this pasture, the ones Slim was supposed to watch. They came in and milled around the pickup, but every now and then they'd hear the wind stir up a strange sound and they'd run off a little ways.

Slim took a bite off his plug of tobacco and studied the cattle. "Hank, it appears to me the coyotes have been prowling around these heifers. They're awful jumpy. I sure hope we don't have a calf-killing coyote on the place. I guess we'd better start carrying the .22, don't you reckon?"

I whapped my tail against the seat. If we had a calf-killer on the ranch, I was betting his name was Scraunch. I'd tangled with that dude before and he was tough. I wasn't exactly looking for opportunities to go against him again on the field of battle, but if it came to that I was ready.

On my ranch, calf-killing is a very serious crime and it demands swift and terrible justice. Slim got out and counted the heifers. They were so waspy that he couldn't get a good count, and after the third or fourth try, he got sore and yelled, "Hold still, dang ya!" They didn't.

Well, Slim had left his window down so I bailed out, thought I might give him a hand. There was a mottle-faced heifer on the edge of the herd, kept running off and acting silly. I started stalking her, and the next time she left the herd, I went into action.

"All right, you old sow," I growled, "that's about all of that stuff we're gonna take from you! Now get yourself back in that herd and stay there!"

By George, that got her attention. She stopped dead in her tracks, snorted, and started shaking her horns at me. A lot of dogs would have sold out right there and headed for the pickup. Me, I don't scare so easy. Sure, she had enormous horns that tapered down to dagger points, but after you've worked cattle for a while, you get to where you can read their minds.

Cattle are basically dumb, don't you see, and heifers tend to be dumber than grown cows and maybe even dumber than steers—which is a little hard to believe since steers are incredibly stupid. You just wouldn't believe some of the stunts they pull.

Anyway, heifers are short a full load of brains by quite a bit and they'll always try to run a bluff on you. They've got this little routine where they snort and shake their horns and beller, and some of them will even paw the ground. I've seen it a hundred times, maybe a thousand.

It's all bluff.

Very seldom do you run into one that does

what this one did. Dang her soul, she ran her bluff only she wasn't bluffing. It's hard to tell sometimes. She came a-hooking, and fellers, it was pretty plain on her face that she intended to put the britches on me.

I held my ground until the last possible second—well, actually until she gathered me up on them horns and pitched me halfway across the pasture, kinda surprised me. When I hit the ground, there she was again, and you know what else? All her dumb friends came charging over to get in on the action. By George, I had forty-seven pregnant women with horns trying to take a razoo at me.

I've said this before but it bears repeating. There's a thin line between heroism and stupidity. Where your ordinary mutt might hold his ground and throw himself into senseless combat, your better grade of cowdogs will make a mature assessment of the situation, realize that nothing is gained from a childish outburst of temper, and then run like a son of a gun for the nearest cover.

No ordinary dog could have reached such a mature decision so quickly or sprinted so fast to the pickup. As you might guess, I did, but it required poise in the face of danger, a great deal of experience, and superior intelligence—not to men-

tion just plain old brute animal athletic ability.

I took aim for the window, and as I leaped high in the air, I looked back at the old sookie and said, "Sister, after you've had that calf and lost about two hundred pounds, you might be able to stay up with me, but . . ."

Looking back on the incident, I'm guessing that the wind must have turned the pickup completely around. There's no other way of explaining why the window glass was rolled up. Through some freak of nature, possibly a giant whirlwind, the pickup had swapped sides and I dived into the window on the passenger side. Never saw anything like it.

I smashed into the glass, just knocked a slat out of my nose, rattled my teeth, snapped my spine, and popped my neck, but the worst of it came when that old barrel-bellied sister got me on the ground.

She wasn't kidding. I mean, if I hadn't crawled underneath the pickup, she would have built a mudhole right in the middle of my back!

Life has many lessons to teach, and even I get sent to school every now and then. The lesson to be learned from heifers is that it doesn't take any brains to be stupid, but just because they're stupid doesn't mean they can't hurt you.

Slim finally got 'em fed but he had trouble packing the bales around because he was laughing so hard, which I thought was just a little tacky. At last his skinny face appeared underneath the pickup and he said, "Come on, Fang, we got cattle to feed. Now don't you hurt those heifers."

Little did he know what I could have done . . . oh well.

We went on to the north pastures and fed other

bunches of ungrateful morons. Slim insisted that I stay in the cab. I consented but only because I feared what I might do if given the opportunity. All the way home, I brooded over my nose, which appeared to be bent to the left.

It was dusk by the time we made it back to headquarters. The snow had slacked off to a few small flakes, but the dull gray sky promised more. The wind died to a whisper and the cold winter night began to creep in.

I went to the machine shed to check on Drover. I found him asleep on a pair of Loper's coveralls (which, I might point out, Loper rarely wore because his cowboy vanity didn't allow it).

"Hey, wake up. We got work to do."

"Huh, what?" He sat up. One of his ears was perked higher than the other, a sign of mental confusion. "Oh, it's you."

"That's right. All goofing off and half-stepping stops as of now. Pay attention, I got two questions for you."

"Wait a minute." He sat there until his ears evened up. "Okay, ask me anything, Hank."

"All right. Number One, did you serve your time in the corner?"

"Corner . . . serve time . . ." He rolled his eyes around. "Oh yeah, gosh yes, Hank, and it was just awful! I didn't think I could stand it."

"Uh-huh. Number Two, whose idea was it for you to serve your sentence *in the machine shed,* where it was warm and dry?"

"It was your idea, Hank, don't you remember? You studied on it for a long time and you decided there weren't any corners outside and I couldn't stand in the corner unless we found one."

"I said that?"

"Sure did. You figgered there were four corners in the machine shed, and you were right."

"Hmm, I'll be derned. Nevertheless, Drover, the sentence wasn't nearly harsh enough and . . ."

Just then we heard Slim down at the house. "Here Drover, come on, boy!"

Drover sprang to his feet. "Uh oh that's me gotta go bye." And in a flash, the runt was gone.

I stepped outside just in time to see Slim and Drover go into a nice warm house for the night.

The Cold Weather Cowdog Blues

Don't get me wrong. Sleeping outside in the dead of winter was no big shucks to me. I mean, my attitude is that if you go into security work, you take the bad with the awful. You take the worst they can throw at you, chew it up, spit it out, and go back for more.

I'd slept in cold, snow, rain, blizzard, sleet, ice, you name it. In my years of security work, I'd slept in everything but comfort, and that was okay because I'd never wanted to be anything but tough.

And as for having someone to talk to at night, I never needed that either. Most of my heavy and dangerous work comes in the night and I never found much time or need for talking on the job.

On the other hand, I'm only flesh and blood. It's

hard to remember that, but it's true. Inside every cowdog there's a heart and a liver and a gizzard— well, I'm not sure about the gizzard, but we definitely have hearts and livers. And where you find a heart and a liver, you'll find the same basic emotions that exist in ordinary dogs.

I mean, we cowdogs have tremendous pride and we have to struggle every day with our emotional side. When you make your living doing battle against evil and darkness, you find it hard to admit that you have feelings. I don't remember who said it, but "Steel crieth not."

Maybe I said it. Even so, it's true.

Steel crieth not.

I'm trying to prepare you for a shocking revelation. On that particular evening, December 22 I believe it was, when I saw Slim and Drover go into the house, when I saw the warm yellow light coming from the kitchen window, when I looked up at the smoky dark sky, when I felt the chill rising from the snow, when I heard the whisper of the wind, when I went down to my cold gunnysack bed—fellers, I didn't feel very much like steel anymore.

I hate to admit it, but I was lonesome and blue. I wanted to be in a warm house. I wanted to see light and hear laughter. I wanted to curl up in

front of that big Jotul stove and watch the logs burn down to red embers. I wanted to hear the rocking chair squeak on the old pine floor. I wanted somebody to reach down and scratch me behind the ears.

I tried to shake it off. I went on patrol and made my evening rounds, down to the cake house, over to the feed barn, the calf shed, the saddle house, the sick pen, up to the chicken house, and then to the machine shed.

Everything was quiet and there I was again, looking down at the light in the window.

I didn't figger there was much chance of me talking my way into the house. I mean, Sally May had been pretty clear that she didn't want "Hank McNasty" in her house, and I think she meant ME when she said that. On the other hand, Sally May wasn't around, and as the saying goes, "When the cat's away the dogs try to get in by the fire."

It was worth a try.

I loped down the hill, hopped over the fence, and took up a position right under the kitchen window. I could see Slim plain as could be. It appeared that he was standing over the sink, peeling potatoes. I tuned up and sang him a mournful song.

Well my bed is cold and I'm feelin' kind of old,

I got the cold weather cowdog blues.
My bones are achin' and my whole body's sha-
    kin',
I got them cold weather cowdog blues.
Don't tell me that I'm a guard dog.
Don't tell me I'm sposed to be tough.
'Cause I'm lonesome and I'm blue and I'm cold
    as a frog
And I just can't handle that stuff
Tonight.

It would sure be nice just to thaw my ice,
And curl up by the wood burning stove.
I got the sleepin' outside, layin' in the snow,
I got the cold weather cowdog,
The lonesome as a hound dog,
The cold weather cowdog blues.
Real bad.

Well, I performed the song (my own composi-
tion, by the way) in the snow under the kitchen
window, and naturally I throwed in some whining
and heavy begs at the end.

Slim was listening. I could see him through the
window, even though the screen was rusted and
had some green paint spots on it (typical cowboy
paint job). Then he left the window and I heard his

boots on the floor. He was coming to the back door.

By George, it had worked!

He opened the door and stepped outside.

"What's wrong, Hankie? You hear some coyotes out there?"

No.

"You miss old Drover?"

No. Well, maybe a little.

"Say, it's cold as a witch's refrigerator out here! I don't know how you can stand this cold."

Right.

"Well, old pup, I've got the solution to that problem."

It takes time but they'll come around.

"Here, try this." It was then that I noticed the smoking frying pan. He scraped the contents into the snow. "I got to fooling around and kind of scorched my taters. That'll warm you up. Night night." He went back inside.

I sniffed his taters, which were sending up gray smoke. Did he say "kind of scorched"? He kind of burned them to a cinder, is what he kind of did, and I'd never met a dog that would eat such garbage. I mean, if he couldn't cook any better than that, he sure didn't need to worry about me begging at his table.

Well, I had no choice but to increase the volume

and intensity of my, uh, presentation, so to speak. I howled. I moaned. I cried. I gave him the full load. This went on for fifteen or twenty minutes, until at last he came back outside.

He leaned against the door jamb and crossed his arms. "Hank, you're making an awful lot of noise."

Yep.

"Is this gonna go on all night long?"

Yep.

"It's pretty cold, ain't it?"

Yep.

"Would it help if I let you come inside?"

Yep.

"Will you dogs stay in the utility room?"

Yep. Cross my heart and hope to die.

"I mean, you ain't one of Sally May's favorite pets."

Nope.

"And she'd skin me alive . . . oh what the heck, come on in."

I shot the gap between his legs and by the time he had the door shut, I was curled up on the rug beside Drover. Drover raised his head and stared at me.

"What are you doing in here?"

"What's it to you? I got my rights. You're not the

only privileged character on this ranch. Just go on about your business and don't try to take more than half this rug."

"Oh. Okay." He went back to sleep. I'm sure he needed it since he'd only logged about fifteen hours of rack time out of the last twenty-four.

Myself, I wasn't sleepy. For a long time I watched Slim working in the kitchen. I could barely see him through the smoke. Judging by the smell, I calculated that he was burning newspaper and cardboard boxes, though I found out later that he was actually cooking another batch of potatoes and a hamburger steak.

He scraped the "food" into a plate and walked into the living room to eat. Well, it got kind of quiet and boring in the utility room. Drover twitched and wheezed in his sleep. I got tired of it and decided to move around a little bit.

I tiptoed into the kitchen and peeked around the corner. There was Slim, sitting in the big wooden rocker in front of the wood stove, eating his supper. I dropped down on my belly and started inching my way toward the living room.

I did this very carefully and Slim didn't notice me until I was at his feet in front of that nice warm stove. He was eating with his fingers and he looked down at me.

"Where do you think you're going, pup? That old stove feels pretty good tonight, don't it?" I whapped my tail on the floor. He tore off a piece of cinderized hamburger and handed it to me. "Here, sink your teeth into this."

I tongued it, gummed it, rolled it around in my mouth, and then, well, spit it out on the floor, you might say.

He scowled. "Why you hammerheaded dog, what's wrong with you?"

What's wrong with me is what's kept me alive all these years: I never eat poison.

"You got no taste." He picked the meat off the floor, wiped it on his jeans, and ate it. Then he wiped his hands on his jeans, pushed himself out of the chair, went into the kitchen, and put his plate and two frying pans into the refrigerator.

He must have noticed that I was watching him. "It's an old cowboy trick, Hank. If you put your dirty dishes in the ice box, they won't get moldy in the sink."

I thought that was pretty sharp. Maybe old Slim couldn't cook, but at least he was clean.

He came back into the living room with two glasses. One had soda pop in it and the other was empty. He threw a couple of hackberry logs into the stove and sat down in his chair again. He took a bite off his plug of tobacco and sat there, one leg throwed over the other, looking at the fire.

He had his soda pop glass in one hand and the empty glass in the other. He drank out of one and spit into the other. I watched him for a long time, wondering if he would get them mixed up. He didn't, and I finally fell asleep.

Then I heard his boots hit the floor. He flew out of the chair and ran into the kitchen and held his mouth under the water faucet.

"Well, I think I'll leave it with you, Hank." He pointed a finger at me. "Now look, dog, I'll let you stay by the fire but if I hear you roaming around and acting silly, I'll throw your tail back out into the snow. You got that?"

Yes sir. I whapped my tail extra hard on the floor.

"Sweet dreams." He went into the bedroom, shucked off his clothes down to his red long johns, turned off the light, and went to bed.

Hey, it was great sleeping there by the warm fire. That was as close to heaven as I'd been in a long time, except that wood floor got awful hard along about midnight. I scratched around and changed positions but I just couldn't get comfortable.

I sat up, yawned, scratched a couple of fleas, and wondered what I ought to do. Should I go out to the utility room and sleep on the rug—and put up with

Drover's wheezing and twitching? Should I roam around the house? Should I hop up on Sally May's sofa and run the risk of getting my throat cut?

No. But there was one last alternative. As quiet as a panther, I slipped into the bedroom, one step at a time. At the foot of the bed, I stopped and listened. Nothing but Slim's heavy breathing—snoring, actually.

I lifted one paw and eased it up on the bed.

Then I lifted the other paw and laid it on the bed. I listened. Nothing. Very carefully, I shifted the weight of my body from my hind legs to my front legs and pulled myself up on the bed. Then I froze and listened. Nothing.

I scooted myself across the full length of the bed until I reached the pillow beside Slim's head. Heck, that was good enough for me.

I closed my eyes and shut her down for the night.

CHAPTER SIX

Rooster J.T.

Slept real good. Sally May had a dandy bed. I mean, it was soft but not so soft that it gave me a backache. Now, the pillow struck me as just a tad too firm. It could have been softer. But all things considered, it beat a gunnysack.

Bunking with Slim turned out to be okay too. He snored and talked in his sleep, but I'll take that any day over Drover's twitching and wheezing.

I woke up at first light, slipped off the bed, and padded back into the living room. When Slim got up, he found me curled up in front of the stove. The house was pretty chilly, so Slim loaded the stove with wood, opened up the vent and the flue, and went back to bed to read *The Cattleman* magazine.

After a bit, I heard him say, "Well, I'll be derned!

Who woulda thought that Sally May and Loper had fleas in their bed? Now, that's one for the record books."

Kind of shocked me too, although I'd have to say that having fleas is not the worst flaw a person could have. I've known a lot of dogs who had them and many of those guys were pretty solid.

Still, it was a little shocking that Sally May had fleas in her bed. She just never struck me as that kind of woman.

Well, the stove started kicking out heat and Slim climbed out of the sack for good. He pulled on his jeans and boots and went into the kitchen. He put some coffee on to boil and took the frying pan and plate out of the ice box and started breakfast.

I couldn't get too excited about sitting through another smoke-out. I mean, Slim's a fine guy, don't get me wrong, but I'd already seen what he could do to a normal, healthy potato and a good hunk of beef, and I figgered it was about time to get back to work.

I headed for the back door. Drover was still asleep. "Roll out, son, we got work to do."

He sat up, cross-eyed and cock-eared, confused and disoriented, in other words his usual good-morning self. He staggered to his feet and bounced off a wall before he finally figgered out where he was.

Slim opened the back door for us. "I'll be out directly," he said.

Drover stepped out into the snow and stood there with his feet together. He shivered and moaned. "Oh Hank, I just can't stand any more of this snow!"

"Sure you can." I gave him a shove with my nose. "Go on, move around, rattle your hocks. You ain't gonna die. Go check the feed barn and I'll take a look at the chicken house, meet you back at the gas tanks in half an hour."

"Oh, my feet are so cold!"

"And the mailman comes by at 10:00. We missed barking at him yesterday and we sure don't want to miss him today. He'll start getting ideas if we don't keep after him."

We hopped over the fence and split up. I sniffed out the machine shed, nothing there, trotted on over to the chicken house, ran into that big red rooster with the green tail feathers. Name's John Cluck, and when he pronounces an S, he whistles.

He was out on the runway between the chicken house door and the ground, shoveling snow with his feet.

"Morning, J.T. How do you like this snow?"

"I don't like it, and I think it's a darn disgrace when the senior rooster has to get out and shovel the darn snow when there's big stout boys in the house that won't turn a tap, is what I think! These darn boys think they ought to sleep 'till noon. Nobody wants to work anymore, just party and chase the girls."

"You see anything suspicious in the night?"

"Yes sir, I think it's darn suspicious that these kids nowadays show so little respect for their elders and expect to sleep all day long. I think that's very darn suspicious."

"Actually, what I had in mind was wild animals prowling around in the night."

"Let me tell you something," said J.T. "I'm not near as worried about wild animals as I am about this younger generation. Who's going to teach 'em to work?"

"You got me."

"Who's going to teach 'em the proper darn respect? Who's going to carry the load when the older ones are gone?"

"That's a problem, all right. So you didn't see any coyotes? I got a tip that we may have a killer on the loose."

He leaned forward and squinted one eye. "I'll tell you the killer's name."

"All right, say it slowly and try not to whistle."

"The killer's name is LAZINESS! The killer's

name is DON'T CARE! The killer's name is . . ."

"Hold up, J.T. Did you hear or see anything unusual in the night?"

"Yes sir, I certainly did."

"You better tell me about it."

He looked over his shoulder and moved closer. "It was right after sundown. I had fallen asleep on my roost. I woke up all of a sudden and I heard it."

"Give me a description, details, facts."

"It was an awful sound. It was a terrible sound."

"Be more specific. Was it an explosion? A growl? A scream?"

"No, it was worse, far worse. Somebody was down in the yard . . . after dark . . . singing."

"Huh? Singing?"

"Yes sir, singing. After dark, in the darn snow, singing."

"Well uh, let's talk about that, J.T. As a matter of fact, I heard it myself and I thought it was pretty good."

"Oh no. It was terrible. That crazy dobber, whomsoever he was, ought to be locked up."

"Guess you're pretty much an expert on singing."

"Yes sir, I am. I love beautiful singing. I love the old hymns. And the world knows where I stand on drunkenness."

"What's drunkenness got to do with it?"

"Sir, whomsoever that was in the yard last night, after dark, in the snow, was DRUNK! They don't fool me, not after all these years. I've seen 'em come and go. They're all sorry and worthless and they got no respect for beautiful music."

"I see. Well, I guess when you ask a chicken for an opinion, you deserve what you get."

"Say what?"

"I said, the younger generation is looking better all the time. Now, if you'll excuse me, I've got work to do."

I stalked away. Dumb bird. What did he know about music? As a matter of fact . . . oh well.

I went on down to the gas tanks and found Slim and Drover. Slim was gassing the pickup, getting ready to make his feed run. Drover just stood around, looking pitiful.

All at once I noticed that Slim was staring at something down by the creek. "Say, that's a heifer. What's she doing in this pasture?"

A heifer in the home pasture? "Come on Drover," I yelled, "we've got a trespasser! Follow me and sound the alarm!"

I shot past Slim and took aim for the heifer. But Slim canceled the mission. "Hank, come back here! Leave her alone. Get in the pickup and let's go take a look at her."

Me and Drover hopped into the cab and Slim drove down to the creek. She was walking and bawling and looking around for something.

Slim chewed on his bottom lip and studied the signs. "Boys, that heifer had a calf last night but she hasn't been sucked out. Bag's swollen. What's she doing in this pasture and where's the calf?"

He watched her for a long time, drumming his fingers on the steering wheel. Then he turned the pickup around and headed for the corral. "I hope I'm wrong, boys, but I got a feeling that we'll find her calf dead in the middle pasture. We may have a killer coyote loose on the ranch."

CHAPTER SEVEN

Murder in the Middle Pasture

Slim caught his horse, pulled on his shotgun chaps, tied a bandanna around his neck, and tied an extra pigging string on the saddle.

He led the horse up to the house and went inside. Drover and I waited by the gate, and Drover started moaning.

"Oh Hank, I just don't think I can run all the way up to the middle pasture. This bad leg of mine . . ."

"Oh for crying out loud, will you quit yapping about your so-called bad leg! We've got a possible murder case here and all you can think about is . . ."

"It's the snow, Hank, I just can't . . . and who's going to bark at the mailman at 10:00?"

"Hmm. Now that's a point, but it's got nothing to do with your bad leg."

"Remember, we didn't bark at him yesterday."

"I'm well aware of that situation, since I'm the one who mentioned it in the first place."

"And since you're the one who mentioned it in the first place . . ."

"Will you shut your yap and let me think!" He did and I did. "Okay, here's the plan. I'll go with Slim. We'll leave you here in reserve."

"Oh drat."

"What do you mean, oh drat? I know what you're going to do. As soon as we leave, you'll be warming your buns in the machine shed. That's fine, Drover, as long as you're up at the mailbox at 10:00 sharp. I want you to meet the truck and give him the whole nine yards of barking."

"I sure will, Hank, I'll be there. You can depend on me."

"Yeah, but for what?"

Slim came out of the house and he was wearing a pistol on his belt. He stepped up into the saddle and we went down to the creek and started driving the heifer north toward the middle pasture. We had a little trouble getting her out of the creek willows, but guess who penetrated the dense underbrush and brought her out.

Me.

We pointed her north and drove her a mile and a half through snow. She was in a nasty mood and made several passes at me with her horns. I held my temper this time. I knew she'd had a bad night with the coyotes and wasn't smart enough to tell the difference between a dog and a coyote.

Slim put her through the gate and we drove her into the middle pasture. Another thing he did, which I thought was pretty slick, he made the sound of a calf bawling. The heifer threw up her head and trotted in a straight line to a canyon southwest of the windmill.

I glanced at Slim. He nodded his head. "She knows where she's going now." We followed her down a rocky ravine.

All at once I saw them: two big gray coyotes eating something in the snow up ahead. I bristled up and went on the attack.

Slim saw them too, and he came right behind me with his horse in a gallop. We flew past the heifer and took after the coyotes. I would have gotten more serious about the chase if Slim hadn't pulled his gun and started blasting. When I heard the zing of the first two bullets, I veered

off to the right and let him have the coyotes.

I mean, I've worked around cowboys enough to know that where pistols are concerned, what they hit ain't necessarily what they aim at. If Slim wanted to empty his gun at those coyotes, that was okay with me. I'd watch from the rear.

Well, he emptied his gun and the coyotes gave him the slip and I watched from the rear. He came back with a tired horse and a face that was red from the cold.

"Well, they got away, Hank, and I don't think

I did any more than scare 'em a little bit."

I could have told him.

He rode over to where the heifer was standing over the dead calf, what the coyotes had left of it, and shook his head. "I guess we'd better drive these heifers down into the home pasture where we can watch 'em a little closer. We can't have any more of this."

I walked over toward Slim. When the heifer saw me, she started shaking her horns and came after me again, chased me around Slim's horse until she finally got tired and gave up.

"Boy, she's in a hostile mood," said Slim. "Better stay away from her. She sure thinks you're a coyote."

We left her there, loped out to the back side of the pasture, and started looking for cattle. Lucky for us, we found them all in two bunches near the windmill. We got behind them and drove them south and put them through the gate into the home pasture. Then we headed back to headquarters.

We got there around noon. Slim went on down to the corral and put up his horse, and I went looking for Drover. Naturally I went straight to the machine shed, expecting to find him sound asleep on Slim's overalls.

I peeked in the door, looked around. It was

awful dark and gloomy in there. "Drover?" I heard him whimper and I stepped inside and went toward the sound. Had to go all the way back to the north end and found him amongst the windmill parts and the electric fence chargers. "What are you doing back here?"

"Oh Hank, they came back! I tried to run 'em off but they beat me up."

"Wait a minute. Who came back and beat you up? Coyotes?"

"No, those stray dogs, Buster and Muggs and the others. I went up to bark at the mailman, like you told me, and they jumped me on my way back. I never had a chance."

"I can believe that." By this time my eyes had adjusted to the darkness and I could see that his hair was mussed in several places and one ear had been chewed on. "How bad you hurt?"

"Terrible! I'm wounded, Hank, I may not make it."

"Can you walk?"

"Well . . . I guess so."

"And you can talk. So if you can walk and talk, what else is wrong?"

"Well . . . Hank, I don't like getting whipped!"

"Nobody does, son, but in this business that's just part of a day's work. Even yours truly has been whipped on a few rare occasions, and if it's good enough for me, it's good enough for you. Move around and let's see."

He limped around. "My ear hurts."

"Is that why you're limping?"

"No. My leg hurts too."

"That leg's a long way from your heart, Drover. I don't think you're gonna die."

"That's easy for you to say. A guy just doesn't get any sympathy around here."

"Sympathy, sympathy, sympathy. There, is that better?"

"I guess it beats a kick in the head."

"That's the spirit. Listen, we got big problems. We've been attacked on two fronts today." I told him about the murder in the middle pasture.

"Oh my gosh! Those stray dogs killed a calf?"

I stared at the runt. "Who said anything about stray dogs?"

"Well . . . I did . . . I guess."

"Son, dogs don't kill calves."

"Never?"

"Never, ever. It goes against our nature."

"But stray dogs . . ."

"Stray dogs, ranch dogs, town dogs, it's all the same. It was a coyote job. We caught 'em in the act."

"Oh, I just thought . . ."

"You thought it was an interesting coincidence that a calf was murdered on the very day we had a gang of stray dogs on the ranch."

"Well . . ."

"You thought you would get a gold star for solving the case."

"Well . . ."

"You thought I hadn't considered the possibility that the dogs might have killed the calf and the coyotes came along later and found the carcass."

"Well, that did . . ."

"You thought that would be a simple explanation."

"Yes, I guess . . ."

"But life isn't that simple, Drover. You can't expect to sit in the machine shed and solve a murder case. You have to get out into the real world, in the snow and wind and cold. You have to check the scent. You have to study the tracks. You have to memorize every detail of the murder scene."

"Oh. I guess I was wrong."

"Indeed you were. There's no particular shame in being wrong, but just don't let it happen again."

"Okay, Hank."

"And always remember: on this ranch, perfect is usually good enough."

"Perfect is usually . . . okay, I think I got it."

"Now, where was I? Yes, we've been attacked on two fronts. We have murdering coyotes up in the pasture and a gang of wild dogs lurking around headquarters. I guess you know what that means."

"Sure do."

"What?"

"Well," he rolled his eyes and looked around the shed, "it means we better sleep in the house again tonight, and maybe go in a little early."

"Absolutely wrong. It means I go up north on a spy mission and you'll have to hold headquarters by yourself. Any questions?"

No questions. He had fainted.

"Wake up, Drover, this is no time to show your true colors. Get up and act like a cowdog." I pushed him up to a sitting position. "Now, any questions?"

"My leg hurts."

"That's not a question."

"Is this real?"

"Yes."

"Would you be pretty mad if I stayed in the house tonight?"

"Yes. Your career on this ranch would come to a sudden end, and it's possible that your life would too. All right, can you handle the situation?"

"No."

"Let me rephrase the question." I gave him a menacing growl and showed him some fangs. "Can you handle the situation?"

"No . . . yes . . . I think . . . maybe . . . I'll try . . ."

"That's better. Well, Drover, I'm fixing to leave on a very dangerous mission. If I'm not back in three days, you can assume . . . well, the worst. I have only one request to make."

"What, Hank?"

"When the wildflowers come in the spring, I'd like for you to pick an Indian paintbrush and lay it on my gunnysack. Nothing big, just one flower."

"Oh Hank, don't say that!"

"It could happen. We must prepare ourselves."

"But I'm allergic to Indian paintbrush."

"All right. A winecup will be fine."

"They make me sneeze too."

"Sunflower."

"They're worse yet."

"The flower of your choice, Drover."

"They all tear me up. What about a toadstool?"

"If a toadstool is the best you can do for a fallen comrade, then so be it. I only hope you can live with your conscience."

"Conscience doesn't make pollen."

"'Conscience doesn't make pollen.' Did you make that up yourself or borrow it from someone else?"

"It's all mine, Hank. You like it?"

"It sounds a little deep for you, Drover. That worries me."

He shrugged and grinned. "I guess I just got lucky."

"I guess you did. Well, I'm off to the canyons. Good luck and be brave."

And with that, I headed off to a new adventure—and possibly to a violent end.

CHAPTER EIGHT

Amongst the Buzzards Again

{{

I lit out from headquarters and made my way through the ice and snow, taking aim for the big canyon country north of headquarters.

My plan, as you might have guessed, was to locate the coyote village and establish an observation post in some rocks or brush nearby. I figgered that with my keen ears and uncanny vision, I could wait and watch and listen until I had assembled enough evidence to locate the murderer.

And then I would face a small problem. Once the murderer had come forward and bragged himself into incriminalization . . . incrimination whatever the word is, I would face the question of what to do about it. I mean, you don't just waltz into the middle of a bunch of wild coyotes and make an arrest.

Coyotes aren't real bright but they can count past one. In other words, they've got enough knowledge of mathematics to calculate the odds in a tussle between one dog and a whole coyote village.

What's more important, I could calculate the odds and it wasn't likely that I would try to make such a foolish move.

That left a certain void in my strategy, don't you see, but in the security business you can only take strategy so far, and then you have to "root hog or cut bait," as they say.

Once I passed beyond strategy, I would have to depend on my keen instincts which had been built up over many years of dealing with riff-raff, criminals, and dangerous characters.

Anyway, with these heavy thoughts weighing heavily on my mind, I headed north into the canyon country.

No ordinary dog would have taken on such a mission. No ordinary dog would have left a warm house and a warm fire and gone out into the snow. No ordinary dog would have ventured into enemy territory with night approaching. But as you might have guessed, Hank the Cowdog has never aspired to ordinarity.

By the time I reached that first deep canyon in the west pasture, the gloom of night had begun to settle across the barren, snow-covered land, and the heavy gray sky was spitting down a few flakes of snow.

It was a night not fit for man nor beets, but onward, ever onward I pushed, deeper, ever deeper into the silent mysteriosity of the canyon.

I was padding through the snow, looking up at the canyon walls, when suddenly my ears flew up. I stopped in my tracks and listened. There it was again! The haunting sound of a coyote singing his evening dirge.

My heart began to pound. The hair stood up on my back. My stomach growled because, well, I hadn't eaten in a while. My ears stiffened to their full alert position. My eyes searched the canyon rim.

Slowly but inexorably, my sensory equipment focused on one spot: a cave in the canyon wall.

I crept toward it, taking full advantage of what little natural cover I could find. The snow crunched beneath my paws. I could hear the singer's voice very well now, your typical coyote singing the day to sleep.

Whether he was alone or part of a large war

party, I couldn't determine. At the moment, I could only hear the single voice.

I slipped from rock to rock and bush to bush and made my way up the canyon wall. As I neared the mouth of the cave, I was struck by an odd sensation—the feeling that I had visited this place before in a dream.

This phenomenon, known as Pre-Visitation Dreameration, is fairly common among the higher echelon of cowdogs. Stripped of the complex scientific language, it simply means that some dogs actually have the ability to visit the future in their dreams—hence my feeling that I had been to this cave before.

The best scientific minds in the world have grappled with this mystery but have failed to explain it. Even I can't explain it. All I can say is that it happens.

I hunkered down among the rocks and listened. Imagine my surprise when I heard a banjo playing! Yes, I had dreamed this scene before, I knew I had. The banjo was poorly tuned, just as in my dream, and the voice . . .

I'm g-g-going to l-leave old T-T-Texas n-now.
I've g-g-got no u-u-use for the L-L-Longhorn
    c-c-c . . . steer.

74

I peered over the ledge and saw—not a coyote, as you might have suspected, but a crook-necked, pot-bellied, banjo-picking, stammering, stuttering buzzard named Junior.

Through some small navigational error, I had ended up at the cave of Wallace and Junior, and if the surroundings had struck me as vaguely familiar, they should have.

I hadn't dreamed about the dadgum cave, I had been there, which confirmed my original suspicions regarding . . . never mind.

Anyone can get lost in that big canyon. It's no disgrace.

I pulled myself over the ledge. I looked at the buzzard and he looked at me. He craned his neck and squinted his eyes, then a smile spread across his beak.

"Oh b-b-boy, it's my d-d-doggie f-friend!"

"So it seems, Junior, so it seems. I see you're still studying music in your spare time."

"Oh g-g-gosh y-yes, I l-like mu-mu-mu-mu-mu-music, and I w-want to b-b-be a su-su-singer when I g-g-grow up. What are y-y-you d-doing h-h-h-here, D-D-Doggie?"

I studied the claws on my right paw for a moment. "To tell you the truth, Junior, I've had this cave under surveillance."

"You h-have?"

"Yes. I'm investigating a murder and you'll need to answer a few questions. Where were you this morning at daylight?"

"D-d-daylight, let's uh s-s-see." He rolled his eyes and pulled on the end of his beak. "M-m-me and P-P-Pa were f-f-flying around, l-l-looking for b-b-b-b-breakfast."

"Ah ha, breakfast! Now we're getting somewhere." I moved closer and began pacing. "Tell me, Junior, on the morning of . . . this morning, did you and your father find any of this alleged breakfast?" He nodded. "Just as I suspected! All right, this next question could be extremely important. Answer it very carefully. What exactly did you and your father eat for breakfast? I want a full description, details, facts."

"Oh g-g-gosh, l-let's s-s-see. W-w-we f-found a p-piece of r-r-rabbit and th-then we f-f-found a d-d-d-dead sk-skunk on the r-r-r-road, and then w-w-we . . ."

Suddenly, I whirled and faced him. "Some dogs might believe that story, Junior, but it won't work on me. I know you know something you're not telling, and you know I know you know it, so let's quit playing games."

I could see that this slashing approach had

worked. He hung his head and shuffled his feet. He was ready to confess.

"W-w-well okay, if you r-r-really have to know."

"I really have to know, Junior. There's nothing personal in this. It's just part of my job. Let's take it from the beginning. You were flying over the middle pasture." He nodded. "You saw something down below." He nodded. "You went into a dive and swooped down on it." He nodded. "All right, you take it from there."

"It was b-b-brown, and w-w-we swooped d-d-d-down on it and w-w-we were so h-h-hungry . . ."

"Yes, yes? Brown, swooped, hungry. It's all fitting into place. Go on."

"And P-P-Pa g-got m-m-mad 'cause it was only a s-s-s-sack of gu-gu-gu-garbage, garbage."

"Huh? A sack of garbage? That's impossible."

"And it was f-f-full of p-p-paper and a ba-ba-banana p-peel and all we g-g-got to uh uh eat was a p-p-piece of a ba-ba-ba-ba-balony sandwich."

"I see." I started pacing again. My mind seems to work faster when I pace. Had I been outsmarted by this buzzard or was he telling the truth? The pieces of the puzzle just didn't seem to fit. I had a piece of rabbit, a dead skunk, a sack of garbage, a banana peel, and part of a baloney sandwich.

They just didn't fit.

I decided to try a different tack. "All right, Junior, for the sake of convenience, we'll assume your story checks out. Maybe you and your old man were clean on this one, but what about other suspicious characters? Did you see anyone else in the middle pasture?"

He nodded. "Uh-huh."

I stopped pacing and whirled on him again. "Just as I suspected! You saw the murderers in the middle pasture but you weren't going to tell me, were you? You were going to hide that crucial piece of evidence, but let me remind you, Junior, that concealing evidence makes you an egg-scissory to the crime."

"Oh g-g-gosh!"

"Yes indeed, which means that you could find yourself in very serious trouble. So," I faced him with a cold sneer, "it's confession time. Allow me to reconstruct the scene. You and Wallace were fighting over the baloney sandwich." Junior nodded. "Off in the distance, you saw two, possibly three figures highlighted against the snow." He nodded. "Perhaps they came toward you." He nodded. "And as they drew closer, you saw . . ." I paused here for dramatic effect. "You saw that they were COYOTES!" He nodded.

But then he shook his head. "N-no, they were d-d-doggies."

"No they weren't, they were coyotes."

"D-d-d-doggies."

"Coyotes!"

"D-doggies."

"Doggies!"

"C-c-coyotes."

I had trapped him, using an old trick of interrogation I had picked up many years ago. The technical name for it is Reversible Argumenterrogation, but there's no reason why anyone outside of security work would need to remember that.

The important thing is that you can use it to trip up a difficult witness, get him going in a straight line, see, and then throw in a different word to confuse him. In that moment of confusion, the truth will just by George pop out. I've seen it work time and time again.

"No further questions," I said. "The prosecution rests its case."

"Uh b-but they were uh d-d-d-doggies."

"Perhaps you thought they were dogs at the time, but subconsciously you knew they were coyotes. My clever line of questioning was aimed at drawing the truth out of your subconscious mind. It did. We're finished—except for one last question."

"Uh-uh okay."

"If you're going to sing and play the banjo, why don't you learn to tune it? I mean, I tuned it the last time I was here and now it sounds just as bad as it did before."

He shrugged. "It s-s-sounded p-pretty g-g-good to m-me."

"Yeah, well there's things about music that buzzards may not understand. Let me see that thing." I picked it up and strummed a G chord. It sounded awful! I twisted the pegs and got 'er tuned up. "How about 'Good Night, Irene'? You know that one?"

"Uh w-w-well, a little b-b-bit."

"I'll do the verse and you come in on the chorus. We'll sing the world to sleep, Junior, just me and you, and then I have to be off on a dangerous mission."

Sometimes I sleep in the cake house,
Sometimes I sleep on the ground.
Sometimes I take a great notion
To jump into the sewer and drown.

Oh Beulah, good night, good . . .

Junior was shaking his head. "Uh w-wait a m-minute, D-D-Doggie, y-you uh g-g-got the wrong w-w-w-w-w-w . . . girl. It's uh su-su-supposed to b-be I-I-Irene, n-not B-Beulah."

"We changed the words."

"Uh okay."

"Start the chorus again, two three, . . ."

Oh Beulah good night, good night.
Beulah good night. Good night Beulah,
Good night Beulah,
I'll see you in my dreams.

I love that girl, God knows I do,
I'll love her till the creek runs dry.
And if that girl turns her back on me
You can kiss that bird dog good-bye.

Oh Beulah good night, good night.
Beulah good night.
Good night Beulah, good night Beulah
There'll be a terrible fight.

Stop your ramblin', stop your gamblin',
Stop makin' patrols at night.
Go home to that gal with the fine sharp nose
And everything will come out all right.

Oh Beulah good night, good night.
Beulah good night.
Good night Beulah, good night Beulah,
I'll see you in my dreams.

On the chorus, old Junior came in and croaked
a little harmony part. Wasn't too bad. When we
were finished, he said, "Who's uh B-B-Beulah?"

I laid the banjo down and sighed. "Well, that's
a long story, Junior. Let's just say that at this
time of the day, when the quiet creeps in and the

shadows grow long, I find myself thinking about her. If things had worked out different, I might be a married man today, with a home and kids and a beautiful collie bride to fluff up my gunnysack."

"Oh g-g-gosh! Is sh-sh-sh-she your g-g-girl-friend?"

"In a manner of speaking, yes, but I share her heart with a certain featherbrained bird dog named Plato. Sometimes I wish . . . ah well, there's no use second-guessing fate."

"I n-n-never had a g-g-girlfriend," said Junior with a shy grin.

I looked at him for a moment. "Yes, I can understand that. I reckon life can get pretty discouraging for a buzzard."

"Y-y-yeah."

"But maybe one of these days . . ."

All at once I heard footsteps behind me. I leaped to my feet, whirled, and stood face to face with a creature wearing a long black robe with a hood on it.

Unless I missed my guess, the Grim Reaper had just walked out of the cave.

CHAPTER NINE

My Dangerous Mission

Grim Reapers don't often catch me so relaxed and unprepared, but when they do I try to make up for it with an especially ferocious barrage of barking.

And that's exactly what I did to this one. I stood my ground, leaned into my task, and by George barked him up one side and down the other, left him with the understanding that you don't sneak up on Hank's blind side and get off for free.

Over the barking, I heard a voice: "Junior, what is all this dad-danged racket out here! Now you tell that dog to shut up or I'm gonna, how can a body sleep around here with, you tell that, shut up that barking, you silly dog!"

"Oh, h-h-hi P-Pa."

Huh? I shut down my barking to a dull roar and studied the figure in the black cloak. Junior was right. It was Wallace, his old man, but I'd like to emphasize that he looked very much like the Grim Reaper, and I mean VERY MUCH, and anyone who saw that black feathered THING sneaking out of a dark cave . . . it was the kind of mistake in identity that any dog would have made under the same . . .

"Say, I'd better warn you about sneaking up on guard dogs like that. A guy could . . ."

He stuck his beak in my face. "You hush!"

"Okay, but let me repeat . . ."

"You just keep talking, pup, and I'll repeat on you and send you home smellin' like fifteen dead skunks!"

"Yes sir."

There's a time for a dog to stand up and be counted, and there's a time for a dog to sit down and shut up. We already know what buzzards do when they get mad. They throw up. They've got a good aim, and what the old man said about fifteen dead skunks was no idle boast. That was probably his menu for the last three days.

After he'd backed me down, he stalked over to Junior. "I've told you once, I've told you twice, I've told you a thousand times, son, your daddy needs his sleep and I can't sleep with all this dad-drat noise!"

"B-b-but P-Pa, we was only s-s-s-singing."

"You can call it whatever you want, son, but it's noise to me and it's past your bedtime and I'm too tired to fool around and you tell that dog to go on home and get out of here." He turned to me. "Don't you have a place to go at night, every time I turn around you're out here keepin' my boy up and raisin' cane in the middle of the dad-danged night," back to Junior, "and you know I need my sleep because I'm having to feed two mouths instead of one, you won't get out into the world and hustle for grub, and this foolishness is fixin' to come to a screechin' halt!" He glared at me. "Right now."

"B-b-b-but P-Pa . . ."

I started backing toward the ledge. "That's all right, Junior, let's don't say anything we'll regret. I got some serious business to take care of anyway, so I'll just ooze out of here and leave you boys to your own devices."

"Real good idea," said the old man, "and the next time you feel a song in your heart, go somewhere else to sing it, hear?"

"I'll sure do that."

As I slipped over the ledge, Junior gave me a sad smile and waved his wing. "B-b-bye, D-D-

Doggie. C-c-c-come b-back sometime."

Old Wallace glared over the ledge. "Yes, come back when you can't stay so long, and bring some supper."

I was very tempted to exit with a slashing, witty reply, but since the old reprobate was armed and dangerous, I decided against it.

Down in the canyon bottom again, I sniffed the air and got my bearings. At last report, the coyote village had been located further north, up the middle branch of the canyon. I lit out in that direction.

The snow crunched under my feet and my breath made steam in the air. It was mighty derned cold, and had I been investigating any crime less serious than murder, I might have turned around and headed for the house. But duty called, and I kept moving.

Must have gone another quarter mile, up where the canyon narrows and the walls go straight up and there's big boulders all around, and that's where I heard voices. I stopped and listened. In the still night air, I heard yipping and howling and whooping and laughing . . . or should I say laughter and yipter and howlter and whoopter?

Anyway, there was no mistake this time. I had found the coyote village.

I crept forward, one snow-crunching step at a time, until I dared go no farther. I took cover behind a huge boulder and slipped around the side until I had a good view.

And there, in a clearing not twenty feet from where I crouched, were twenty of the most dangerous coyotes in Ochiltree County.

This was the same tribe of wild nomads I had once lived with when, in the folly of my youth, I had considered becoming a wild dog and an outlaw. I had adopted their culture and language and had been on the point of committing marriage with the chief's lovely daughter, Missy Coyote, when I had returned to my senses and discovered an ancient piece of cowdog wisdom: cowdogs and coyotes don't mix.

We're natural enemies, born on different sides of the law, and as the old saying goes, "Never the twangs shall meet." Exactly what a "twang" is, I never figgered out, but I will say this. If a guy was ever tempted to forget his twang and throw in with a bunch of stinking savages, he'd do it for Missy Coyote.

And understand, this observation comes from a seasoned professional cowdog who doesn't ordinarily allow himself to be distracted by women. So there you are.

I studied the faces down below and recognized several of them. There was old Chief Many-Rabbit-Gut-Eat-in-Full-Moon, the rowdy brothers, Rip and Snort, and over on the edge of the crowd . . .

Mercy! My old heart was made of cast iron but derned if it didn't start acting silly when I saw her lovely face. Missy was just as pretty as I'd remembered her. All at once I got weak in the legs and swimmy in the head, and there for a minute I thought that wicked old heart of mine was going to take out a couple of ribs, it was pounding so hard.

Old Chief Gut was seated on a rock, telling a story about . . . couldn't hear every word so I kind of had to patch it together. Sounded as if the story came from his youth, back before he got old and crippled up and lost two toes in a fight with a badger and got a notch bit out of his left ear.

The story had something to do with running a jackrabbit. It must have been funny because every now and then the whole bunch of 'em would bust out laughing—everyone but Missy. Over on the edge of the crowd, she smiled but didn't laugh. No doubt she'd heard the story several dozen times already.

That was one thing about Old Man Gut I remembered. His stories were pretty good the first time around, but the third, fourth, and fifth times they got a little stale. But you know what? His poor old wife laughed every time, just as though she'd never heard them before. Now that's real devotion.

I was focused in on Missy's pretty face when all at once it struck me that someone was missing: Missy's brother Scraunch, the meanest, boldest, strongest, dangerousest, chicken-killingest, rotten-meat-lovingest coyote in the whole village, and perhaps the entire world.

I mean, Scraunch was BAD NEWS, fellers. I knew because I'd tangled with him on several occasions and I'd been lucky to escape with my life and both ears intact. I didn't exactly cherish the idea of going against him again, but he was a prime suspect in my investigation and I had to find him.

It was also kind of crucial that I spotted him before he spotted me. The element of surprise can be very surprising when the other guy uses it first. In going against Scraunch, I would not only need the element of surprise but other elements as well, such as plain old luck.

I searched the faces in the crowd again, just to be sure I hadn't missed him. Sure enough, he wasn't there.

Where could he be? Had he died in battle? Had the tribe run him off? Or was he at that very moment down in the home pasture, stalking some poor innocent calf and plotting another dastardly murder?

Yes, of course! Suddenly it all fit together. I had fallen for the oldest trick in the coyote book of old tricks. I had been duped and lured up into the canyons, while the villain Scraunch had slipped down to headquarters to kill another calf!

How could I have been so dense, so easily fooled! I had taken the gambit and now . . . I had to get back down to headquarters, double-quick, or else I would have another murder on my hands.

I turned to leave . . . and looked right square in the sharp-nosed, yellow-eyed face of Scraunch the Terrible.

Confused, Captured, and Condemned

"So," said Scraunch in a deep and cruel voice, "we meet again at last." And he was grinning. Did I mention that? Yes, grinning, which sort of unnerved me.

"Yes indeed, we meet again at last," I managed, trying to keep my voice from cracking. "It's been a long time."

"Long time Scraunch dream revenge-make on Chicken Dog."

"On whom?"

"Chicken Dog."

"Oh, I guess that means . . . uh, me, you might say." His head moved up and down. "I thought maybe that's what you meant. You always did call me Chicken Dog, didn't you?" He nodded. "I never

did care much for that name, Scraunch, but by George if that's what you want to call me . . . Listen, I know you probably have a few questions to ask me, but I think I can explain everything."

His head moved from side to side. "Scraunch not have question."

"Oh. Not even one? Well, in that case, maybe you could give me one small piece of information."

"Scraunch not give information."

"It's very small, tiny, little bitty. I was wondering where you were on the night of . . ."

"Chicken Dog not talk. Chicken Dog march into village."

"Into the village. That's, uh, right over there, I guess you mean, where the rest of your thieving . . . uh, your kinfolks are, is probably what you're saying, but I have another suggestion, Scraunch. Would you consider . . . now I know this is going to sound a little outrageous but hear me out . . . would you consider going down to headquarters with me and answering a few questions?"

He raised his lips and showed me his teeth. It was a good set, long, white, and very sharp. "Chicken Dog want die now or later?"

"Is there a third choice?"

"No third choice."

"Well, in that case uh . . . let's save it till later."

"Move!"

"All right, all right." We started down to the village. I considered making a break for freedom, but with Scraunch right behind me I knew I wouldn't stand a chance. He would have been on me like a duck on a junebug. I had to play for time, pick up all the information I could, and hope that a miracle might save me.

(I might point out here that hoping for miracles wasn't a common cowdog stratagem. I had seldom used it in my work, but then I had seldom found myself in such a mess.)

"Say Scraunch, you know what would really hit the spot right now? A nice warm piece of veal. You had any good veal lately?"

No answer.

"You're a very serious fellow, Scraunch. Anybody ever tell you that it's hard to carry on a conversation with you?"

No answer.

"The trouble with you coyotes is that you've got no sense of humor. Were you aware that too much seriousness can cause cancer?"

No answer.

"I guess not."

No answer.

"And furthermore, you probably don't even care."

No answer.

"One more small item, Scraunch, and then I'll be quiet."

"Be quiet!"

"Okay, I can handle that."

We marched into the coyote village. When Chief Gut saw me, his mouth froze open and he stared. The rest of the coyotes turned and stared. A rustle of whispers spread through the crowd.

A smile bloomed on Chief Gut's mouth. "Ah ha! Oh foolish dog to walk into coyote village on cold cold night. Berry berry foolish you come back."

I walked up to him. "Thanks, Chief Gut, and it's great to see you again too. Listen, I can't stay long but while I'm here, I'd like to say a few words to your people."

That must have caught him by surprise. Before he could say anything, I turned to the crowd.

"Ladies and gentlemen, children, honored guests, members of the committee, Madame Secretary, Chief Gut: It is indeed a pleasure for me to be here tonight to accept this honor. It's impossible for me to tell you how much this means to me . . ."

Out of the corner of my eye, I could see Chief Gut staring at me with a kind of perplexed look. Then Scraunch came over and they conferred in low voices.

I went on talking. I mean, what else could I do? I was buying time.

"I probably don't deserve this award, and as I stand before you tonight, I'm reminded of all the dogs who helped me along the way. Without their help and encouragement, I wouldn't be here. So let me pause here to thank them all: my mother, my father, my brothers, my sisters, my uncles, my aunts, my cousins, my second cousins, my grandmother, my . . ."

Chief Gut came over and cut me off. "Hunk not understand. We not give award."

I looked at him. "What?"

"Hunk not understand. We not give award."

"What?"

He cleared his throat and raised his voice. "Hunk not understand! We not give award!"

"What!"

He took a big gulp of air and bellered, "HUNK NOT UNDERSTAND! WE NOT GIVE AWARD! AND HUNK BETTER CLEAN OUT EARS AND LISTEN!"

"No award? Are you serious?"

"Berry berry serious."

"Hey, wait a minute, hold everything. I was told that I had been voted Dog of the Year."

The chief went back to Scraunch and they held another conference. I could hear them muttering. Scraunch appeared to be a little upset. Chief Gut came back to me.

"No. We not have Dog of Year award. We not like dog."

"You mean I came all the way into this canyon for nothing? After I went to the trouble of walking here in the snow, you're not going to give me my award?"

"That right. No award."

"Well I never . . . This is an outrage! This is a crime against decency! I demand a recount!" Gut shook his head. "Very well, if that's the way you want it, that's the way it'll be. You leave me with no choice but to walk out of here in disgrace. So good night, ladies and gentlemen, good night members of the committee, I'll be going."

I hoped they might be so surprised by this craziness that they would let me go. The coyotes in the audience seemed confused about it all, and they whispered back and forth. Chief Gut shook his head and tried to explain to his wife what was going on. I stalked off the platform and threaded my way through the audience.

I had almost made it to the other side, where I could turn on a burst of speed and make a run for the ranch, when I heard Scraunch's booming voice: "Halt! Stop that dog!"

Suddenly two big bruisers stepped into my path and showed me their teeth. I recognized them: Rip and Snort, my semi-pals. In better days, we had been singing partners and drinking buddies. Unfortunately, I had pulled a few nasty tricks on them and I wasn't sure just how solid a friendship we had.

"Hi, fellers. Any chance you'd let me pass?"

They shook their heads. "I guess you're working for Scraunch now, huh?" They nodded their heads. "And probably the good times we've had together don't amount to much." They shook their heads. "So the bottom line is that I'm sort of trapped?" They nodded.

I turned around and marched back up to the front.

"Ladies and gentlemen, may I have your attention please. I have a very important announcement to make." The crowd fell silent. Over to my left, old Gut was still explaining things to his wife. I turned to him. "Sir, please. I've asked for silence. Ladies and gentlemen, members of the committee, honored guests: Because of circumstances beyond my control, I have no choice but to reveal my true identity and tell you why I am here tonight."

Dead silence. Every yellow coyote eye was locked on me.

The following information will probably shock you. It might also frighten some of the children. I ask that you remain calm, and at the conclusion of this shocking announcement, you should rise and go quietly back to your homes.

"Ladies and gentlemen, I have penetrated your security apparatus and infiltrated your village for one purpose: I am here to arrest one of your tribesmen on the charge of calf murder."

The crowd buzzed at that.

"Now, if you will turn the guilty party over to me and return to your homes, we can settle this matter without violence and bloodshed."

I waited for someone to name the murderer. Instead, some yokel on the front row started laughing. The laughter spread like a grassfire in a high wind. Within seconds, the entire coyote village was roaring—everyone, that is, but Missy. She had her head twisted to the side and there was a puzzled smile on her lips, as if she were thinking, "What is this dog talking about!"

Well, the laughter went on for several minutes. Them coyotes were falling on the ground, rolling on their backs, kicking their legs in the air, slapping each other on the back, the whole nine yards. In other words, they had misinterpreted my announcement.

Chief Gut came up on the rock and whopped me on the back. "Berry good, yes, Hunk berry funny. We not laugh so much in long long time."

"Well, thank you, Chief. You've been a wonderful audience."

"Oh how funny, joke about we kill calf."

"You liked that one?"

"Oh boy, funny funny, because we not kill calf."

"Huh? You . . . well, of course I knew . . . are you sure about that?"

"Wild dogs kill calf. That berry berry funny to coyote."

That got the crowd in an uproar again. They laughed and howled and slapped the ground.

At last the pieces of the puzzle had fallen into place. I had suspected all along that Buster's gang of wild dogs had been behind the killing, but I'd had no proof. Now I had my proof. My mission was a success and I had solved the case.

"Well, thanks for everything, Chief. I guess I'd better be getting back to the ranch."

"Oh no! We have big celebration at sunrise."

"Really?"

"Yes, big BIG celebration. You stay."

"Maybe some other time."

"You stay!"

"Oh what the heck, I'll stay. What are we celebrating?"

"We celebrate Hunk die when sun come up, oh boy!"

Oh boy, my foot! Fellers, I was in trouble up to my eyebrows, and I didn't know how I was going to get out of this one.

CHAPTER ELEVEN

Locked in a
Dismal Cave, Escape
Impossible

Scraunch raised his paw and Rip and Snort came to take me away. They marched me off to a dismal cave in the side of a cliff. As I was leaving, I caught a glimpse of Missy.

Her face was an island of sadness in a sea of merriment.

Rip and Snort threw me in the cave and sat down in front of the opening. I sat down several feet away from them. I couldn't situate myself any farther back because there was a packrat's nest at the rear of the cave.

As you might know, packrats build a mound of cow chips, sticks, pieces of sagebrush, and so forth,

and then cover the mound with cactus petals. I
didn't need any cactus in my tail, thank you.

For a long time we just sat there staring at
each other—they with the kind of dull, brutish
expressions you would expect in dull, brutish coyote warriors.

Well, I had to make a move, and fast.

"May I ask a personal question?" No response.
"Have you guys ever considered taking a bribe?"
They shook their heads. "There are many advan-
tages to a well-planned bribe program. You ought

to think about the future, your families, what happens when you're gone."

No response. "I think we could work out a real fine program. Let's see now. How do you feel about dog food—kernels, very tasty, wonderful stuff?" No. "All right, let's talk about bones. We could probably come up with a dozen of the smelliest bones you ever saw." No. "I'd let you bathe in my sewer. I mean, I'd be willing to throw that in as an extra."

No deal. These guys weren't too smart but they were double tough.

"All right, forget the bribes. Let's talk about the brotherhood of all animals. I'm sure that strikes a responsive chord . . ." They shook their heads. "Or maybe it doesn't. Okay, let's put all the cards on the table. I'm in a jam, fellers, I need to get out of here. Can you think of any way you might let me escape?"

They shook their heads.

"You don't have to decide right this minute. I don't want you to make any hasty decisions. Take your time, think it over, and . . ." They shook their heads. "What about the good times we've shared? The singing, the laughing. Isn't that worth . . ." They shook their heads. "You guys are heartless, do you realize that?" Yes, they did. "Just big hairy shells without hearts or souls or . . ."

I noticed that their eyes were glazed, and suddenly I realized how I would make my escape. Why hadn't I thought of it before?

Degenerate characters like Rip and Snort couldn't be beaten by direct force. I mean, fighting was their game. They could fight from daylight until dark and get stronger and meaner by the hour.

But I had hit upon the hidden flaw in their psychobasical whatchamacallit—their personality, I suppose you could call it, meaning the personality of your basic dull brute. The flaw was that they couldn't stand preaching. It put them to sleep!

Give them something to fight against and they would stay up for days, maybe weeks. But give them a good wholesome sermon to listen to, and within minutes they would be reduced to snoring wads of hair.

It was a brilliant stroke. I could hardly contain my excitement. I launched into a sermon.

"The trouble with you guys is that you don't spend enough time doing good and spreading sunshine. Have you ever thought about how wonderful this world would be if every one of us tried to be wonderful all the time?"

Their eyelids drooped. Rip yawned.

"Just imagine how much better the world would be, Snort, if you concentrated on doing good.

Instead of drinking and carousing and fighting and staying out all night, you could spend your days looking for the good deeds, the little acts of kindness . . ." I went on and on.

I stopped and studied my victims. By George, it had worked! They weren't just asleep, they were comatose. Now all I had to do was step over them, slip out of the village, and high-ball it back to the ranch.

I rose to a crouch and crept forward. They were snoring so loud, their lips were flapping on the exhale. Perfect. Very carefully I picked up my feet and placed them in the open spots amongst the pile of legs. I had almost made it when, dang the luck, I stepped on Snort's nose.

He came out of sleep like a wounded panther. I dived to the rear of the cave, expecting to be mauled. Snort snarled, his teeth flashed, and he tore into his brother.

"Not step on nose again, dummy, or Snort make big hurt!"

They growled and snapped at each other for half a minute, grumbled for another minute, and went back to sleep. But this time Snort wasn't sleeping as soundly as before. Every few minutes, he would crack one eye, look at me, look at Rip, and go back to sleep.

My time was slipping away. I figgered I had maybe one more hour before sunrise. I didn't relish the thought of walking over that pile of deadly fangs again, but sooner or later I would have to try it.

I waited for my chance. I listened to them snoring. Felt kind of sleepy myself, had to concentrate hard on
keeping my eyes
open
and staying
A
   W
     A
       K
         E

                ZZZZZZZZZZZ

I went to dadgum sleep. My last night on earth, one hour before my execution, and I couldn't stay awake!

Next thing I knew, they were getting me up. Outside, I could see the first light of day. I looked up into that coyote face, realized that I had muffed my one chance to escape, and felt a cold shudder pass through my body.

"No, wait a minute, let's talk about bribes again . . ."

"Sh-h-h-h-h! Hunk not talk! Must hurry and run away!"

"Huh?"

The face above me came into focus. It wasn't Rip. It wasn't Snort. It wasn't Scraunch. It was Missy Coyote!

"Missy, what are you . . . how . . ."

She placed her paw over my mouth. "Come, follow Missy."

I soon learned how she had managed to enter the cave. There was a secret passage at the rear. I hadn't seen it because it had been covered by the packrat's nest. Coming in from the back side, Missy had simply dug her way through the cowchips and cactus petals and sticks and pieces of sagebrush.

We dived into the tunnel and must have crawled twenty or thirty feet on our bellies. At last we came out into the fresh air. We were standing on a bluff above the village.

I looked into Missy's face. A gentle north wind tousled her long winter hair. "Why did you do it, Missy?"

"Not want to see Hunk die. Hunk save Missy once. Now Missy help Hunk."

"You're quite a woman, Missy." Also very attractive. I couldn't take my eyes off that gorgeous face. "Do you suppose this might lead to something in the romance department? I mean . . ."

"Hunk run away! Must hurry, village wake up soon."

"Oh, they might sleep a little late this morning. I sure could use a big old sloppy kiss."

"Not be foolish! Scraunch bad bad fellow, he kill!"

"Listen, gal, the way I feel right now, I just might go down there and slap your brother baldheaded. In fact, I think I could whip the whole family."

Down below, someone shouted. Then there were other voices.

"Hunk, go, please go!"

"Missy, it'll take 'em a while to get percolating. We've got time. Now give me one little old sloppy kiss."

She puckered up and I puckered up and our lips met in an outburst of flaming desire, and then she BIT me. And I ain't talking about a little nip, fellers, I mean she got a handle on my lower lip and played meat grinder with it. Just bit the tar out of it.

I yelped. Who wouldn't have yelped? It hurt.

"Run away, foolish dog!" Then she leaned out and pecked me on my bleeding lip. "But come back another time, oh boy!"

"Oh boy, you can depend on that! Bye, little darlin', and thanks for everything!"

I struck a high lope and headed south down the canyon. In the distance, I could hear Scraunch shouting at his warriors and telling them to hunt me down. Still, I couldn't resist stopping and looking back one last time.

There she stood on that wind-swept hill, waving good-bye. All at once I decided what the heck, I'd go back for one last kiss, didn't figger old Scraunch could get his boys whipped up and on the trail for another ten or fifteen minutes, only he did and the thought of being torn to shreds right there in the snow overpowered my appetite for a kiss.

I turned on the speed and went flying down the canyon, with Scraunch and his boys hot on my trail.

As I passed the buzzard cave, I caught a glimpse of old man Wallace. He stuck out his skinny neck, looked at me, looked at the coyotes right behind me, and started jumping up and down.

"Junior! Git outa that bed, airborne, airborne, our breakfast is runnin' down the canyon!"

That's the kind of friend a buzzard makes. There's always an ulterior motive.

The old man hopped off the ledge, flapped his wings, and crashed into the snow, and I didn't have time to see what happened next, because them coyotes were closing the gap on me.

Leaping over rocks and bushes and fallen trees, running through deep snow, and doing things no ordinary dog could have done, I flew down the canyon, leaped the water gap between the west pasture and the home pasture with a single bound, scrambled up an embankment, and lit out across the rolling prairie country, taking dead aim for headquarters.

I could see it up ahead, maybe a mile away. A coil of white smoke was coming out of the chimney, which meant that Slim had throwed a couple of fresh logs and last Thursday's *Ochiltree County Herald* into the stove and was probably taking his dirty frying pan out of the ice box.

If I could just get down close to the house, I could sound the alarm and old Slim would save my bacon. He'd come out the door in his red long johns and start blasting away with his pistol. If he didn't shoot me by mistake, I'd be home free.

I glanced over my shoulder at the Coyote Nation. I had a good fifty feet of cushion and I figgered I could coast on in to headquarters without any trouble. Them boys sure looked unhappy about the situation. I guess they was a little shocked by my incredible speed and unbelievable endurance.

I turned my eyes back to the front and was very surprised to see four dogs lined up between me and the house: Buster, Muggs, and the other two gangsters.

They were coming out to help me. Receiving help from calf-murderers raised a few ethical questions in my mind but none that I couldn't dispose of pretty quickly under the circumstances. I mean, dogs is dogs and coyotes is coyotes, and there's a certain bond that ties us dogs together when a brother is in danger, regardless of our moral, religious, ethnic, socioeconomic . . . well, all of that stuff that makes us different.

In other words, blood is thicker than coyotes, and when the chips are down, I don't remember the last part of the old saying.

"Boy, am I glad to see you guys!" I yelled.

For some reason, Buster let out a wicked laugh. "You won't be for long, cowdog. I'm taking over this ranch."

HUH?

Come to think of it, they didn't look too friendly. No, they sure didn't. That's why their teeth were showing and their eyes sparkling with a murderous gleam.

Hey, those guys weren't coming out to help me. They were coming out to GET me!

Another Amazing Conclusion

I was by George trapped, is what it amounted to, between a pack of murdering wild dogs and a pack of murdering wild coyotes.

Now, I could have whipped one group or the other. I mean, odds of four- or five-to-one were nothing out of the ordinary for me. In security work, we figger four-to-one is about a fair fight, five-to-one is a challenge, and six-to-one is a pretty good scrap.

"One riot, one cowdog," is the way we put it.

But I hadn't been training for seven-to-one, and the chances of me whipping and possibly annihilating both groups were pretty slim.

Very slim.

Out of the question.

Which made retreat an attractive option, except

there was no place to go. I stopped. Buster and his boys stopped. Scraunch and Rip and Snort stopped. The coyotes glared at the dogs, and the dogs glared back at the coyotes.

Scraunch broke the silence. "Hunk belong to us. We not need fight everybody, only want Hunk."

That gave me an idea—the only one I had left, as a matter of fact. "Did you hear that, Buster? He said you guys better pack up and get off this ranch. And in case you don't know it, he's a very important official in the coyote tribe—no less than the son of Chief Many-Rabbit-Gut-Eat-in-Full-Moon."

Muggsie started laughing. Within seconds, they were all laughing. "What kind of two-bit foreign name is that! Many-Rabbit-Gut! Har, har, har!"

I turned to the coyotes. "There's your answer, Scraunch. Buster says you guys are a joke and you'd better vanish before there's a big fight."

Rip and Snort might not have understood every word of this, but they did savvy the word *fight*. And all at once their eyes lit up and they started whispering.

Buster took a step toward me. "Why don't you shut up. I can talk my own fights without any help from a yellow-bellied cowdog!"

"Did you hear that, Snort? He told you to shut up, and then he called you a yellow-bellied cowdog!"

The hair went up on Snort's back, and he took two steps forward. "Snort not like big talk."

Buster's eyes moved from me to the coyote. "Oh yeah? Well let me tell you something, pal. Me and my boys got some business to take care of, so why don't you just shove off?"

Snort and Buster glared at each other. Then Rip stepped out and swaggered up beside his brother.

Buster grinned. "Oh yeah? Hey Muggs, come here." Muggs moved up beside Buster and curled his lip at the coyotes. "Give 'em a growl."

Muggs puffed himself up and let out a deep growl. Rip and Snort looked at each other and started laughing. I mean, those guys had been in so many fights, the idea of running a bluff was a joke.

That didn't sit too well with Buster. "Wise guys, huh? Ho-kay, whatever you think." He looked back and jerked his head at the other two goons. "Come here, boys. We got a couple of wise guys here." The two dogs came up and took their place in the line. Buster turned to Rip and Snort and grinned. "Now, like I was saying, why don't you guys go chase a rabbit and we'll tend to our business, huh?"

It was a stand-off. Both sides bristled and glared and snarled and stared, but neither one made a move. Then Scraunch came up. "Not need fight with many dog, only want . . ."

Buster's head shot around. "Yeah, I bet you don't want fight with many dog, Chief-Chicken-Guts-in-the-Moonshine."

Muggs broke up on that. "Har, har, har! Chief-Chicken-Guts, har, har, har, in-the-Moonshine, har, har, har!"

Snort's eyes bulged. "Not laugh at Scraunch!"

"Oh yeah?" said Buster. "Listen, pal, we're taking over this ranch and my boys can laugh at anything they want, see? Go on, Muggsie, laugh for the bumpkins."

"Har, har, h . . ."

That was one har too many for Snort. If you recall, he wasn't a real bubbly sort and had a lousy sense of humor. He piled into Muggsie, Scraunch lit into Buster, and Rip took on the other two. And fellers, the fight was on!

Snow was flying, hair was flying, teeth were flashing in the sunlight. It took my coyote pals maybe thirty seconds to clean house on them junior thugs. I mean, you talk about a *whipping*! Buster and his boys got a very quick and very painful education on pasture fighting.

Buster was the first to put his education to good use. About thirty-five seconds into the fight, he broke away and went tearing down the county road, with Scraunch right behind him, taking a snap out of his tail every five steps.

When Muggs and the others saw their fearless leader running for his life, they tried to surrender. But Rip and Snort were just getting tuned up and didn't care about taking prisoners, so Muggs and the boys broke away and lit a shuck down the county road, with Rip and Snort in hot pursuit.

"That's what we do to calf-killers!" I yelled. "And the next time I catch you on this ranch . . ." They had already disappeared. That was the end of that.

I headed down to the house and met Slim and Drover in the pickup. They were coming out to the pasture to see what all the noise was about. Slim had his gun. I was real glad he didn't get a chance to use it.

"Hank, what in the world . . . we thought we'd find you dead up here. What did you do to those brutes?"

What could I say? One riot, one cowdog.

"Good dog, good dog!" He got out and rubbed me behind the ears. "Get in and let's go check the heifers."

Just then I heard a voice from heaven: "Dang the luck! There goes our breakfast, Junior!"

I hopped into the cab and sat down beside Drover. He stared at me with eyes as big as saucers.

"How's it going, son?"

"How'd you get out of that? You're not even hurt!"

"Oh, I just read 'em the law, told 'em what was likely to happen if they stuck around here very long."

"You just . . . no foolin'?"

"You saw the results. Need I say any more?"

He scratched his head. "I guess not."

We checked the heifers, didn't find evidence of another murder, and Slim was kind enough to give me the credit I so richly deserved.

Then we went back to the house. I got double dog food and for the rest of the day I was treated as a conquering hero and resident dignitary. I accepted it graciously, even though it was long overdue.

That night was Christmas Eve, and old Slim was feeling so generous and full of holiday cheer that he let me and Drover into the house again. In fact, he let me occupy the place of honor in front of the stove.

He'd cut a scrubby little cedar tree up in the canyons that afternoon. He set it up in a corner, and after he'd burned himself some supper, he started decorating the tree.

He cut some pretty pictures out of a magazine and tied them on with string. He wedged some apples and oranges against limbs and hung his spurs out on the ends of a couple of others. Then he took his foil chewing tobacco pouch and made a star out of it, and he put the star right up on tippy top of the tree.

Then he stood back and said, "What do you think, Hank? I believe we've got ourselves a Christmas tree."

Looked okay to me.

Just then, we heard a knock at the door. Slim frowned and said, "Wonder who that could be," and opened the door.

"Surprise! We decided to come on home." Loper stepped inside and started stomping the snow off his boots.

Instead of going back to his little house down the creek, Slim bunked out on the sofa and I curled up on the rug in front of the stove.

It was a joyous, old-fashioned, cowboy kind of Christmas, the best Christmas I'd ever known. There was only one small incident that marred what was an otherwise lovely occasion.

Around nine o'clock on Christmas morning, Sally May found fleas in her bed.

Even though Slim had occupied that bed for several nights, guess who got blamed for the dadgum fleas. I was banished from the house.

But I couldn't complain. A guy can't expect to sit on the precious moments of this life and hatch them out into something better.

In the security business, you make your own bed and sleep in it. Every once in a while you have to expect a few fleas.

Join Hank the Cowdog's Security Force

Are you a big Hank the Cowdog fan? Then you'll want to join Hank's Security Force. Here is some of the neat stuff you will receive:

Welcome Package
- A Hank paperback of your choice
- An original Hank poster (19" x 25")
- A Hank bookmark

Eight digital issues of *The Hank Times* newspaper with
- Lots of great games and puzzles
- Stories about Hank and his friends
- Special previews of future books
- Fun contests

More Security Force Benefits
- Special discounts on Hank books, audios, and more
- Special Members Only section on Hank's website at www.hankthecowdog.com

Total value of the Welcome Package and *The Hank Times* is $23.99. However, your two-year membership is **only $7.99** plus $5.00 for shipping and handling.

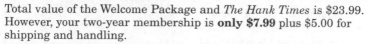

☐ Yes, I want to join Hank's Security Force. Enclosed is $12.99 ($7.99 + $5.00 for shipping and handling) for my **two-year membership**. [Make check payable to Maverick Books. International shipping extra.]

WHICH BOOK WOULD YOU LIKE TO RECEIVE IN YOUR WELCOME PACKAGE? CHOOSE ANY BOOK IN THE SERIES. (EXCEPT #50)   (#   )

_____

YOUR NAME   BOY or GIRL
                                             (CIRCLE ONE)

_____

MAILING ADDRESS

_____

CITY   STATE   ZIP

_____

TELEPHONE   BIRTH DATE

_____

E-MAIL   (REQUIRED FOR DIGITAL HANK TIMES)

Send check or money order for $12.99 to:

Hank's Security Force
Maverick Books
P.O. Box 549
Perryton, Texas 79070
Offer is subject to change

DO NOT SEND CASH.   NO CREDIT CARDS ACCEPTED.
ALLOW 2-3 WEEKS FOR DELIVERY

Photo Courtesy of Western Horseman Magazine

John R. Erickson, a former cowboy, has written numerous books for both children and adults and is best known for his acclaimed *Hank the Cowdog* series. He lives and works on his ranch in Perryton, Texas, with his family.

Gerald L. Holmes has illustrated numerous cartoons and textbooks in addition to the *Hank the Cowdog* series. He lives in Perryton, Texas.

Shawn Tevis Photography

And, be sure to check out Hank's official website at
www.hankthecowdog.com
for exciting games, activities and up-to-date news about the latest Hank books!